White Zombies of New Castile

This time travel mystery is based on the author's belief that Christopher Columbus discovered America on a secret first voyage that took place before his official and well documented voyage of 1492. No other interpretation, says the author, who has studied the life of Columbus over a period of many years, explains all the known mysteries, queries and questions regarding Columbus and his fraudulent claim of discovery under the flag of Castile. This is the mystery of the man who stole two continents, North and South America, in two different ways − (1) legally from his former sovereign and (2) physically from its former owners the Amerindians.

The story is told from the point of view of Dr. Solomon Cohen, who tells the story of how he and close friend, the Antiquarian, time travel back to 1500 A.D. where they sail the Spanish Main. There they investigate the alleged crimes of Columbus, who was at that time Viceroy and Governor of the New World as well as Admiral of the Atlantic. All characters, and major situations, although based on true life, have been entirely fictionalized. In this time travel mystery, do the Antiquarian and his friend solve the mysteries of the great explorer?

Well, it's a strange story . . .

LIFE OF DREW CARSON

Sam Drew Carson was born in the North of Ireland and educated there at Wellington College and the Ulster Polytechnic. He completed his education in the USA at New Mexico Highlands University and the University of Arkansas and has traveled widely in North America, around the Atlantic and in Europe.

Drew worked as a seaman and fish-gutter in Vestmannaeyjar off the coast of Iceland. He lived and worked in the Irish and Western Isles Gaeltachts and was married in Welsh-speaking Carmarthen after which he honeymooned in Belfast.

He has told his stories, composed and sung his songs, seeking storylines in Bristol and the English Westcountry. Drew has also lived and written in Nashville, Tennessee, in the wooded hills of Mid-America and from the Appalachians to the Ozarks. This was the culture that gave rise to the now worldwide Scotch-Irish country music.

In the USA, he also worked beside the bayous of the French-speaking Cajuns in the South and among the Western Spanish-speaking Navajos, Apaches and Pueblos of the Sangre de Cristo Mountains in New Mexico.

Drew has sailed far into the seas of old Gaelic and Oriental legend. After many years searching for inspiration for story and music, the author is still traveling and writing.

BOOKS BY THE SAME AUTHOR

ZENISUB
Fun and Games in Businezz
ISBN: 978-0-9561435-2-5
GOOD FOR A LAUGH
Six Funny Playscripts for Amateurs
ISBN: 978-0-9561435-3-2
HOME WITH A GOOD COMPANION
Amateur Pantomime Scripts for a Merry Winter
ISBN: 978-0-9561435-4-9
CLASSIC EUROPEAN LYRICS
Translated from the Gaelic, the French and Spanish
ISBN: 978-0-9561435-6-3
COMMONWEALTH
An Introduction to Business Economics
ISBN: 978-0-9561435-7-0
WEREWOLF MURDERS
Detective Felix O'Neill in a Crime Adventure
ISBN: 978-0-9561435-9-4
ORIENTAL GOVERNESS
Detective Felix O'Neill in a Crime Adventure
ISBN: 978-1-908184-00-9
EASTER AND THE SPRINGTIME
Five Amateur Playscripts about New Life
ISBN: 978-1-908184-02-3
WALLWAVE THE YOUNG SEA WARRIOR
Adventures of War Queens and Battle Heroes
ISBN: 978-1-908184-03-0
WALLWAVE THE SEA PRINCE
Adventures of War Queens and Battle Heroes
ISBN: 978-1-908184-04-7
WALLWAVE THE SEA KING
Adventures of War Queens and Battle Heroes
ISBN: 978-1-908184-05-4
THAT SILVER SHORE
Easter Musical with Ten Songs
ISBN: 978-1-908184-06-1

THE OTHER SIDE
Halloween Masque of Demons and Delusions
ISBN: 978-1-908184-07-8
SEE YOU AROUND
Pantomime of Bygone Fun and Frolic
ISBN: 978-1-908184-08-5
CULT OF THE WIDOW VIDOVA
Detective Felix O'Neill in a Crime Adventure
ISBN: 978-1-908184-09-2
WHITE ZOMBIES OF NEW CASTILE
A Sci-Fi Adventure
ISBN: 978-1-908184-10-8

WHITE ZOMBIES OF NEW CASTILE

A Sci-Fi Novel

DREW CARSON

Legals

ISBN: 978-1-908184-10-8

TABLE OF CONTENTS

MAIN CHARACTERS IN THE MYSTERY

THE ANTIQUARIAN/BOBADILLA –

An historical investigator now in the guise of a nobleman of Castile, who is sent out by the King and Queen to investigate the alleged crimes of the Governor of New Castile.

DOCTOR SOLOMON COHEN –

The investigator's close friend now in the guise of a ship's sawbones.

PRIMO –

The former assistant of the Governor, El Gringo. The Governor had cheated the poor hidalgo, Primo, out of a just and promised reward. He hopes to bring El Gringo to justice and loathes the man who cheated him.

EL GRINGO –

The Governor of New Castile who is accused of wrongful floggings, hangings, theft of taxes, stealing gold, treason to their most Catholic majesties.

THE KING AND QUEEN –

Ferdinand and Isabella, sovereigns of Castile who had sent out El Gringo, in the first place, to explore and find a new world. They, too, need to judge El Gringo.

Chapter One

The Antiquarian Discovers
an Old Mystery

The antiquarian engages in a deep study of Admiral of the Atlantic and Governor, Christopher Columbus and concludes that there are many unanswered questions about the Admiral.

Seahaven fog? Are there visions and old dead dreams in the Seahaven fog?

This is the chronicle of an adventure undertaken by the antiquarian and his friend and physician, Dr. Solomon Cohen. This mystery must rank as not only one of the most outlandish events that my friend and I have ever experienced in our many years of acquaintance but surely as the most unusual journey ever undertaken by anyone in any time or clime known to man.

This is a fantastic claim to make but no more fantastic than the story itself which spans hundreds of years, thousands of miles and the fate of two continents, North and South America.

It all began one evening when I made my usual visit to my long-time friend, the antiquarian, who was always engaged in researching some area of history that caught his attention. On this particular visit I noticed with approval that he was throwing himself into the unsolved enigma of Christopher Columbus, the discoverer of the Americas.

Of course, I knew from my schooldays that Christopher Columbus presented many unexplained puzzles to the historians but I never suspected that these mysteries were so many, so deep, so intractable as to dumbfound the mind of one of the most illustrious historians, my friend, the antiquarian.

So it was that one day, as I returned from my evening surgery, I was astounded to see him down on his knees on a rug in his study and library with well over 50 old books, maps and letters lying open before him on the carpet. He was examining with his magnifying glass these tools of olden lore – many old and faded, some in strange type or in Spanish or Latin. Some were slim pamphlets while others were huge volumes of historical accounts, memoirs and folklore.

Gingerly tiptoeing through the open books so as not to disturb any, I found an armchair beside the open bureau bookcase and gratefully lit a Havana. I have always made a point of never drinking in my surgery, that is to say my consulting rooms.

As I took a deep breath and reached for my decanter and glass, I noticed from the cold tea sitting on his desk that he had not been drinking for some time so fascinated was he with the floor spread with papers and books. Indeed, he was so intense in his pursuit of answers that he seemed to be almost, if not quite, unaware of my presence. I was very pleased about this and smiled to myself with the thought that he was far from entering into one of his self-destructive weed-puffing fits of agonized boredom.

So it was that after a few minutes of contemplative relaxation that I cleared my throat pleasantly and in a quiet tone designed not to suddenly distract my friend from his research.

Still busily on his knees he smiled and looked up as one coming home from afar.

"Ah yes, there you are, my dear friend, all these memoirs, maps, collections are index fingers pointing to what is one of the greatest mysteries of all time – Who or how or why was Christopher Columbus? What was his secret? I think we know the what, where, when or do we?"

"Really," I responded, "wasn't he simply the navigator who discovered America?"

"He was that but how much more than that," he replied as his eyes glinted coolly with a hard faraway gaze.

"Yes, so much more than a discoverer. He was a man of no known origin – forget Genoa – he was not born there. His true name is unknown. On his first discovery voyage, in 1492, he knew precisely when the New World would come into view.

"A penniless foreign adventurer, he had great power over King Ferdinand and Queen Isabella and received a munificent deal from them. Dogs played a large part in his life."

I relaxed more into my armchair, sipped on my glass of wine as he got up from his knees, sat in his comfortable old rocking chair and took up a large Cabernet Sauvignon.

From where I sat I could read some of the large gilt titles stamped on one or two of the huge volumes on the floor and these I read aloud with curiosity.

"Great Dog Breeds of the World - Worldwide Ghosts, Demons and Monsters - Encyclopedia of the Supernatural and My Voyage with Christopher Columbus."

I also noticed one of my own current favorite books lying on the floor among the others – Folk-wisdom and Proverbs of all Nations.

"Tell me what have dogs and ghostly monsters to do with Christopher Columbus?" I asked in surprise.

"Irish wolfhounds and zombies seem to be a big part of the Columbus mysteries but what part exactly I'm not quite sure. To solve these enigmas and puzzles one would need to go back in time and that is impossible, at least within the present state of our sciences."

"Quite, but my dear friend," I replied, "I have always been more inclined than you to believe in ghosts and indeed monster stories. You're the skeptic."

He knotted his eyebrows together in a gesture of frustration and I sensed a slightly defensive, even embarrassed, tone in his answer.

"Of course, that's so. I do not believe in ghosts as you put it but there's more to it than just believing or not believing in ghosts. The ghost story does not primarily ask us to believe anything but it can in a sense act as a signpost to the unanswerable.

"The underlying idea of the ghost story is to make people think about the things of the spirit. The ghost story is rarely didactic; rather it provokes the reader's mind to ask questions about God or gods, the devil or demons, the place of the human psyche or mind or soul in the events of our universe. It is designed to query, to question and to suggest ideas rather than to provide hard and fast answers and to provoke thought and philosophies rather than dogmas but sometimes to throw light on dogmas.

"First of all, we must postulate that a good ghost story is not just scary rubbish. A good ghost story is a stimulant to forming creative and original ideas about the abstract universe around us as opposed to Newtonian or Einsteinian mathematical models.

"Some ghost stories call upon us to elucidate our relationship with our abstract past, present or future. Sometimes the ghost story throws light on power relationships between humans. It questions who is dominant, who is subservient and who is manipulative as between persons? Sometimes it asks: What of one's relationship with oneself?

"Other ghost stories lead us to think in one or another direction that we might not otherwise consider to be in touch with reality. Often, but not always, ghost stories query, try to explain or provoke alternative ideas about our lives, ideas that may well be in contrast to the shibboleths of institutionalized religions.

"Often ghost stories ask poetic questions like: What is spiritual reality? What is the next life? Is time a clock that runs forever – can it be put back and reset? What is eternity in relation to time? How do we enter it? What is heaven or hell? Do our souls move from one netherworld place to another?"

I listened with delighted interest to his astonishing short dissertation on the supernatural. It was only at that time that I came to realize fully, although I had long since suspected it, that despite my friend's outer crust of skepticism and hard scientific method, underneath it all he was fascinated with all kinds of mystery, both worldly and spiritual. I felt that this went some way to justify my own long-term interests in magic and the occult.

As I ruminated upon his abstract, ethereal ideas and eternal questions, he and I seemed to find ourselves moving onto a misty higher plane. It was as though we had jointly entered a dream already well in progress. We were our usual selves in essence and yet perhaps not quite ourselves . . .

The ground began to sway and undulate under our feet. It was as though we had partly merged into the personas of sailors on the Spanish Main. The warm blue seas lapped around our ship – an oldtime sailing bark with the cross on its sails.

We looked at each other and shrugged in mystification for some time and then I ventured to speak first.

"What on earth are we doing here?" I asked.

"My dear friend, I believe we are here to investigate – to pursue an enigma – perhaps the greatest one in modern history – the Mystery of Christopher Columbus."

It was the early 1500s. It was as though we stood unsteadily on the focsle of a stout, broad ship, something like the famous ship of Christopher Columbus – the Santa Maria.

My friend was dressed as a Spanish

gentleman of high rank and I was dressed in the humble uniform of ship's surgeon – a crude sawbones in those days – but at least I was with my friend the antiquarian.

*****

Chapter Two

The Investigator

An investigator is sent out by the King and Queen to find out if El Gringo is committing murder, extortions, thefts and enslavement of Christians. Primo, the Governor's former assistant, has been assigned as an informant to the investigator.

The antiquarian was his usual self, at least in essence but he was also an emissary of the King and Queen of Old Castile and their appointed investigator. His high military helmet was a stern frame for his lean, hawkish face and he looked a fit commander of the ship *Holy Savior*.

He was acting in the persona of one Bobadilla, a Castile gentleman of high rank. He was also sophisticated and of ancient and distinguished lineage.

I was now also playing a duel role as a mere ship's sawbones.

We had been sent across the seas to sift out credible allegations of cruelty, slavedriving, murder, corruption, and withholding wages.

These allegations had been made against the foreign adventurer who had somehow mysteriously wormed and squirmed and weasled his way into the position of governor in an imperial province.

As Bobadilla and I stood on the brow of the ship, I looked around to survey some of his high-ranking navigation officers. They were far from noble or even clean – dirty, swarthy, rough-spoken and surly. The only exception was his first officer, Primo, a Castile hidalgo.

I began to think about El Gringo and how he had risen to such a high position.

I wondered aloud, "How do these upstarts get the jobs when those truly qualified are left hanging around with two arms the same length?　Isn't this the perennial question of the refined, the just, the masterly, the honest and the educated?"

"Surely," Primo spoke up, "Satan is the God of this world; surely Satan sabotages God's work, with the eager approbation of perverts masquerading as God's people.　Surely the Good Lord will return one day to set aright all such misrule."

"Perhaps so," Bobadilla replied, "but in the meantime one must not assume the guilt of anyone."

I nodded in agreement as my friend continued.

"Rather, all must be investigated impartially.　Although witnesses of good repute have already testified to El Gringo's corruption and his cruelty, it really remains to be seen who exactly is responsible for precisely what."

Bobadilla, the Castile gentleman, then more kindly addressed the hidalgo, a retainer of modest rank.

"Primo, sit here and share some wine.

Now that we have been at sea for many days and have almost completed our voyage - you have no doubt observed that there are some islands to the west of us - we shall have more time for you to tell me about this foreign upstart .. this . . ."

"Yes," Primo responded eagerly, "Yes sir. I was with the foreigner, the upstart criminal, on his so-called voyage of discovery - discovery! What a joke - the devil had told him where and when and what he would discover. Believe me, Excellency, I know enough about the gringo to hang him if there is any justice in the world."

Bobadilla replied, "Primo, I'm afraid in this world we can look only to a limited degree of justice."

"Just so, Excellency - that is why I say if there is any, any justice at all, even to a limited degree, the criminal known as El Gringo must be hanged . . ."

"Quite, Primo. Quite. But we must probe and prove the case carefully and fully before we adjudge guilt or innocence. Their most Catholic majesties demand as much and will in any case make the final judgment of guilt or innocence."

"Innocence - hah, hah - don't even think of it, your Excellency. That vile low born bandit is a murderer and a liar by profession."

"But Primo didn't you tell me that he is of unknown origin?"

"Exactly. He is an upstart foreigner, your Excellency."

"I agree with you that he is not from the city he pretends he comes from as his birth records are not in that city. Also he has often changed his name. To hide what I ask you?

"But if you don't know from whence he came, how can you know that he was low born, perhaps he is an aristocrat of some far off unknown land, right?"

"Your Excellency, I served with him; he does not act like a gentleman. He comes from a vile and evil clan I am quite sure of it."

I interjected at this point, "Know the breed and know the dog." I quoted reflectively, "But you are arguing the reverse."

"Yes," Primo agreed. "El Gringo has

no code of honor or truth - he is a cheat, a liar, a bully, a murderer, a slaver - so I assume that he is low born."

"That does not necessarily follow," said my friend the antiquarian. "There are high born cowards and low born heroes. And, of course, many high-born Castile nobles have supported El Gringo."

"You will see in just a little while as we approach these islands your Excellency how few support him except that mercenary rabble who would murder for money. They are the mob from the lower regions who support him but few others. There are always those, at any rank in life, who will do anything for wealth. Such is El Gringo and such are his supporters - anything for money and power."

"Primo, I am aware of the basic charges made against El Gringo. Murder, slavery, theft, torture, cruelty and so on. Yet you were with him a long time - when and how did these crimes begin? Try to be calm and unprejudiced Primo. I chose you as my companion for your knowledge of the upstart, El Gringo, not for your hatred of him. I need not to hate but rather to know, to investigate and to find out the truth."

Primo cast his eyes down but more in despair than shame.

"Your Excellency, to know El Gringo is to hate him. It cannot be avoided. His dishonest deeds stir up only contempt in the decent human soul. Listen your Excellency, I swear to you on the blood and the life of Mary the mother of heaven that my testimony is totally true and not a word of a lie."

A fleeting, not unkindly smile flashed briefly across the face of the antiquarian/ Bobadilla, the aristocrat. His left hand briefly flicked something away - a fly, a thought, an idea, a culture? Who knows?

"No, no, Primo. Such fearful oaths are the stock in trade of those who expect to be disbelieved. Just tell me simply and straight . . ."

"Master, you are right. I do, I really do expect to be disbelieved totally - but not because I lie - only because the truth is so frightening, so strange, so horrific.

"It is like this, their most Catholic majesties promised nobility and wealth and recognition to the first man to discern land. Why? What land? What were they expecting? So, it so happened that I saw land first. I was that man. I saw their land afar off. I cried out 'land.' True enough El Gringo, in league with Satan no doubt, seemed to know when land would appear. And for sure he forewarned me."

"Now Primo, how could he have known what no man ever knew before. No one had ever sailed these seas before El Gringo. How could El Gringo have known when land was about to appear, Primo?"

"Yes, your Excellency, El Gringo knew almost within minutes certainly within hours when to expect land. That is the proof that El Gringo uses magic - the gift of the devil - to achieve his ends."

"Primo, you are a Catholic and you believe in the greater power of good to overrule the devil. Your voyage with El Gringo was on behalf of their most Catholic majesties. I do not believe that magic ruled your voyage to the least extent. There must be a better reason."

"But your Excellency there is no better reason than magic."

The great antiquarian waved his hand in a curt gesture of dismissal. "Primo, I will not hear of it. Forget it." He shook his head. "Magic indeed."

"Very well, your Excellency. Just as you say. Yet there are many witnesses to the fact that El Gringo knew when to expect land."

"I keep trying to tell you I have no doubt of that, Primo. I have heard other good witness to that effect. But we must find a better explanation than magic. You understand?"

"Of course, Excellency. But at any rate I was the first to see the land, and the Admiral, the foreigner, the great liar and cheat, the upstart heard me call 'land' and sent me below and then he himself began to cry 'Land,' 'Land.'

"I sat there stunned and unable to comprehend what was happening just as I sit here now penniless and no noble. Just as I was born a mere hidalgo - a landless esquire, a respectable but penniless gentleman, a retainer of my betters - all as a result of the upstart's, El Gringo's, lies and usurpation of my position. I was the true discoverer of these islands.

"I well remember the day he stole riches and fame and titles for himself and threw me into the trash-heap of poverty, misery and nonentity . . ."

I sighed and resorted to my long-studied repertoire of maxims once more. "Hard work will guarantee a living but not a fortune."

Primo was in a trance, his eyes fixed on the past but he gave me a curt nod and then continued his story to my friend.

"But your Excellency, it was a day like today. It was a cool breezy morning not far from the beautiful island here that we are approaching when El Gringo landed his ship here.

"There the island lies - a long, low tropical isle of great luxuriance and bloom. Indeed, it arises out of the sea like one of the fabled Islands of the Blessed or as some say - the Isles of the Young, long written of, and believed in, by the Gallegos. Close to shore we will soon see the colored fish in the sea. On shore there are many gentle green slopes with all kinds of trees and bushes and grasses and foliage. Meadows of many flowers, fruits of all shapes and colors mingled with herbs and fragrances and tingling smells . . .

"The sweet corn thrives on friendship with man. The air is clear and fresh - not one of all our crew had a headache or catarrh or drowsiness. Our minds were sharp and enjoying the peak and energy of life - as the ancient Gaels seemed to know - the Isles of Youth indeed. We all felt young and vigorous among the herbs and grasses and bushes and flowers and blooming trees and bees.

"We were all invigorated by small singing birds and strong smelling vegetables like tomatoes and potatoes and grains and nuts such as we had never known before - it was like the Garden of Eden, your Excellency," cried Primo.

"Rabbits in the bushes; dolphins in the sea; lizards in the pools of leaves - all on that paradise - a long, low tropical isle of great luxuriance and bloom. Colored fish there were in the sea and on the gentle slopes of the shore grew all kinds of intricate trees and foliage. Flowers there were a plenty amidst fruits of all kinds and form and color.

"There were also harmless barkless wild dogs to eat the carrion. Also there were song birds, subtle herbs and sweet smells of fruits and grasses and sea vegetables and climbing plants to eat.

"The air was gentle and clear, neither too hot, nor too cold, nor sultry. There the spring and stream waters were transparent and good to drink.

"As we went ashore on this wonderful island, the hypocrite who was later to rob me of my reward as discoverer, kneeled down on the grass to thank God for his find. What an insult to God. Does he think that God is a liar and a thief or in the business of rewarding liars and thieves. O yes, let me tell you how God and I, both liars and thieves, got together to steal from Primo his just reward, says El Gringo. What blasphemy.

"Anyhow, your Excellency, a few grumblers and mutineers implored and were given pardon by the upstart."

"That at least showed Christian mercy, you must admit, Primo."

"Not at all, your Excellency." Primo's

voice was surprisingly hard and gritty. "Not at all."

"No?" queried Bobadilla.

"No, certainly not," he replied. "It was an act of mere shrewdness and cunning. In a little while all of us were to be hard driven like slaves and our gold stolen, so out of crafty greed he pardoned some to use as pawns - the more slaves the better. Also, the foreigner did not wish to show his hand at that early stage or the whole crew might have mutinied.

"At this point the great deceiver wished to receive, indeed he demanded, deference and loyalty from his Castile crew so as to maintain the discipline of the officers against the crewmen and then stealthily and gradually introduce his system of enslavement of both Castile and Indigenos.

"Likewise his form of religion was merely a ruse to fool the crews into subjection and to steal their wages and gold with the advantage of surprise. O yes - who would expect such thefts from a supposedly devout Catholic?

"I well remember how he planted the

Castile flag and named one island New Castile and another Holy Savior and another nearby isle - Holy Mary of the Conception. Who would have expected the carnage, the lies, the lusts, the thefts, the murders that were to be perpetrated on the men of Castile and on the golden bronzed Indigenos on these holy-named islands."

"Yes Primo," I once more put in my twopenceworth, "it is a true saying - You can self-protect from a thief but not from a liar."

Primo ignored me and bowed to Bobadilla.

"Yes indeed Excellency and there stood the great liar, El Gringo, lofty and scarlet-coated, like a cardinal above his priests, towering over the Castile sailors who were dressed in mail, helmets and weapons. But his color red was a sign of the blood he was to shed in cruelty and wantonness, albeit in the name of God and every holy saint he could think of to use as a camouflage for his greed. Ah, why does God permit such evil to dwell on the earth, your Excellency?"

"That is merely to ask, why does God

permit man to dwell on the earth - a good question, Primo, but one that, alas, I cannot answer."

"It is just as you say, your Excellency, man is evil but especially El Gringo."

"Quite Primo, let us say that all men are murderers at heart. We wish to see all others die so that we alone can be the survivor. We gloat in death and the disease of others but it should not be so. However, there are things that I need to find out about this mysterious foreigner.

"Where is his true homeland? Why did he keep changing his name? What is he hiding about his early life? No one knows anything about his early life or names. No doubt he is a great sailor, a dealmaker and visionary. So why should he hide his past?

"Why did their most Catholic majesties offer him 10% of all the wealth he might find when many men of Castile would have undertaken the voyage for one tenth of one percent? Why offer nobility and royalties to his heirs forever when many a great Castile sailor would have done the task for so much less? Above all, how did the upstart know where to expect to see land?

"There is a great mystery here, Primo. I will not accept magic as an explanation but I mean to get to the bottom of it, with your help. You were here before, so where should we start?"

"Your Excellency, let us go ashore and step on this beautiful island of Holy Mary. Here we will find water, food, shelter and for the most part, friendly natives."

"You are sure, Primo - mostly friendly Indigenos?"

"Certainly, Excellency."

"Hmm. Then why does El Gringo continue to bring out savage dogs to drive those natives away? The mystery certainly deepens."

"Excellency, the new dogs of this new world are barking in the twilight. Barking dogs were unknown before El Gringo brought out his hated Irish wolfhounds. That's why the natives fear our loud dogs of destruction."

*****

Chapter Three
Omens

As they near the land of the New World there are three omens of bad luck that presage ill for the expedition.

As the ship *Holy Savior* settled smoothly into the small harbor, a great black crow landed on one of seven jetty poles and cawed and mocked and screeched at the incoming craft. A sailor threw a stone directly at the omen of bad luck but the crow flew up in the air briefly and then landed down on the pole top again to continue its tirade.

Later, after dusk, the royal investigator and his landing party walked from the beach a little ways inland. The foliage was heavy and moist and sweet smelling and hung high overhead. In the distance, dogs barked savagely and howled at the moon.

This reminded me of an ironic proverb: "May the lord preserve the moon from the dogs."

I quoted this to my friend to which he replied.

"Indeed it is a true saying that the dogs howl at the moon but she goes on her way serene."

Soon, the howling of the dogs approached the investigator's party and again some of the seamen had to hurl rocks at the black-coated curs in order to drive them off.

Primo shook his head gravely, "That is bad luck, Excellency."

The investigator looked unpleasantly surprised. "What? What on earth is bad luck?" he asked in puzzlement.

"First the crow, then black dogs come out of their holes in hell to argue with us and dispute our right to be here. Mark my word Excellency, these things go in threes, a third black creature will come upon us to speak to us and warn us of ill-tidings and bad luck ahead. Our pilgrimage to Truth is doomed."

"Primo, these are only senseless animals. They know nothing that we do not know . . ."

Primo raised his eyebrows and shook his head in a shrug that somehow turned into a shudder.

"Well perhaps it is only my superstition to fear bad luck. Yet I hope that I am proven to be wrong, your Excellency."

I addressed Primo cheerfully, "My dear hidalgo, pray. Pray - not hope - it is better to pray than to hope."

"Just so Doctor," agreed Primo with a bow. But he did not speak with any great enthusiasm.

My friend's conversation became a little more light and cheerful as he realized that some of the subalterns and other junior commanders were listening and showed signs of nervousness. Both the antiquarian and Primo, the hidalgo, were well aware of the superstitious murmurings among the junior officers and seamen to the effect that El Gringo was the darling of the fates and that no weapon would prosper against him.

El Gringo was one of the illuminati, one of the chosen few, for whom the pages of knowledge and the doors of destiny would always be opened.

The investigator addressed Primo, the hidalgo, thoughtfully, "Look, Primo, I'm sorry that you were not raised to the ranks of the nobility. I am a gentleman of some rank and I would not wish to be robbed of that status as it means privilege and privilege means that opportunities open up. People obey one. One tends to grow rich and this is all fine and fruitful as far as it goes. But look at it like this, El Gringo was not born a noble. Nobles are those who are lucky for a while. Eminent for a day, often followed by a downfall that lasts till doomsday.

"You see Primo, I am here to investigate the eminent one. Nobles are like castles on the mountaintop. Everyone sees them upon the hill and all attack them.

"Often the King or Queen or viceroy

do not like what they see from their hill. The high powerful barons and dukes may join together and take over the Kingdom, putting a new puppet on the throne. Rich nobles must be brought low and only death is low enough to make sure that they do not threaten the King. One moment nobles are high and mighty, the next moment they are high and headless.

"The humble gentleman is neither a castle baron nor a hungry peasant slave. The middle road is surely the safest, Primo. Nobility has its obligations - to set a good example to others, to please the King - the price of failure is the gibbet, the scaffold, the pyre. Low ranking gentlemen but rarely pay such a high price for they are scarcely noticed, as they go along their happy paths of life minding their daily tasks unthreatened by the jealousies of either high or low, unnoticed by the pauper or the prince. The middle road is surely the most safe, the happiest and the one with longest life."

"Perhaps," agreed Primo, "It is as you say. There are enough good foods and fruits and sunshine in this green haven of the seven seas."

"Primo, I agree, we see here before us such a great wealth of free food from the sea and the jungles. What red and rainbow sunsets. What balmy breezes, Primo, to cool you as you lie in your hammock eating sweet fruit, freely picked. Right?"

"Well, Excellency, that is just fine after a hard day's work supervising the Africans in the hot sun of the gold and silver mines. But why should settlers who are already millionaires still carry on driving poor slaves day after day? Why grab more and more and more money for ever and ever?"

"Well, Primo there is an old saying, Since when has money been a cure for greed?"

At this comment, my friend looked at me for confirmation as I am usually the one to come up the appropriate quotation. I gave them both a smile of agreement and then he continued.

"Need ends soon but greed goes on forever. Yet I agree with you, Primo, there is no need for greed. The good book says, Greed is the root of all evil."

"And when people here agree with you, Excellency, and try to take life easy and retire with their justly and fairly earned wealth, the Admiral and Governor - the great liar tyrant, the foreigner, the viceroy of hell . . ." Primo forgot his train of thought for a moment.

"El Gringo?" I ventured.

"Ah . . Yes, Dr. Cohen, El Gringo hauls the settlers into jail, accuses them of lotus eating, by which he means laziness, and has them whipped or tortured if they are lucky or if they are unlucky then . . ."

Primo drew his hand incisively across his throat and made a choking sound.

"Or burnt alive," he added.

"Well Primo, let us then open up the way for less greed, less slavery, less taxation, less punishments and more just reward for work well done to both rich and poor. More lotus-eating as the Admiral would say.

"Look at those colors, surely those are the greens and blues and reds and pinks of a sky in paradise. While it is still dusk keep an eye out for a place to camp in this strange smelling jungle."

Faintly a dog still howled, far into the darkening woods. My friend and I listened to the uncomfortable sound.

"Listen, Bobadilla," I said with a smile, "Beware of strange dogs and other people's children.

"Also it is often said, Where the river is shallowest it will make the most noise."

Soon we came to a clearing where the grass and bushes had been battered down.

"I think this is a good place to camp, your Excellency," remarked Primo.

"Yes, hidalgo. Indeed, I see that three of our countrymen have made this fine place their permanent home. This is your third black-speaking creature, Primo. You were right."

Primo looked puzzled but turned and followed the upward gaze of the royal investigator.

The small exploratory party drew back in horror. Three Castile noblemen swung heavily from trees, their tongues and eyes bulging, their faces black. All three had been hanged in full Castile uniform of mail and armor. A slight breeze groaned through the gallow trees so that it seemed as though the hanged noblemen moaned. Several sailors made the sign of the cross. Others were too terrified to move and addressed the investigator with hints of retreat.

Even Primo was cautious, "Your Excellency, I have had an idea - perhaps we should spend the night aboard our ship. Just to be watchful and wary."

Bobadilla answered curtly, "We'll camp here. Cut them down. We'll bury them tomorrow. Meanwhile organize a watch."

As though in agreement or in mere obedience, the three noblemen groaned and hung and swung around in a circle, all blind and dead and lame, the brain destroyed. They would never stalk the New World again. Unlike some brethren of the dead who walked the woods unknown.

*****

Chapter Four

The Accused - A Flashback

The antiquarian begins to reminisce and marvel at El Gringo's swift and unexplained rise to power.

Bobadilla did not sleep but rather supervised the watch as they patrolled around the outside of their camp. He remarked that none of the designated watchmen showed any tendency to sleep but the others in the advance party did take the opportunity to snatch some slumber. We were tired and fearful of the unknown so that sleep was not only a rest but a hiding place.

Hand on sword, Bobadilla walked the rounds of the watch and brooded on the strange circumstances which had brought them all to an earthly paradise which had been turned into a subhuman hell by one man - El Gringo.

With an eye on my friend, I admonished myself with the maxim, Work for the night comes when no man can work.

My friend paused in his brief patrol and stared at the three corpses - all three were Castile noblemen. How could such high-born noblemen have been so martyred and in full Castile armor and accoutrements? Surely there must have been a terrible crime committed to justify such a terrible punishment?

And yet, Bobadilla had barely finished assuring Primo that noblemen were liable to be executed merely because the unstable Governor was afraid of being overthrown.

No doubt El Gringo was troubled in his mind, so perhaps the three dead men had done little or nothing but offend the governor. Who was this man who ruled these islands with a red rod of iron, who must have ordered these three fatal punishments? Who was this man? Who on God's earth, other than the man himself, could know the answer to this question? He has changed his name so many times that he could be anyone from anywhere.

Christopher means one who crosses over to Christ and is a Christian name often given to a convert from Judaism or Mohammedanism. Colum means a dove and signifies peace. Supposedly a Genoan, as judged by his accent, yet the family books and bibles of his namesakes in Genoa showed no record of him. As for accents, they can be misleading or even faked.

Yet, my friend Bobadilla mused, this great foreign one, El Gringo, was able to shake the very foundations of Castile in order to get the huge expenses needed for his voyage of discovery. How did he do this? No doubt by presenting their most Catholic majesties with a great deal, a great business offer that they could not refuse. But what offer? It was a deal that was at first rejected and surely seemed very speculative but then there is more to everything than appears on the face of it.

A light breeze from the ocean blew

across the camp causing the sleepers to curl a little more snugly into their capes. The royal investigator turned up his collar as he strode among the sleepers, three of whom would not awaken until the day of doom. Why were both Indigenos and Castile rebelling so fanatically, even at the cost of their lives, against El Gringo?

Yes, my friend Bobadilla reminisced, El Gringo had always been quite a mystery perhaps he was destined to become one of the great mysteries of all time. For who could explain his sudden rise to success? A virtually penniless seaman, supposedly a Genoan, presents a business plan to the King and Queen of Castile. The plan, untried and unproven, is naturally rejected outright by their most Catholic majesties.

Then suddenly and surprisingly, for no obvious reason, the wild, crackpot scheme is supported by high ranking clerics. Then out of the blue, again for no obvious reason, the decision was reversed and the scheme was avidly accepted by the King and Queen of Castile, despite the fact that their majesties were known to be almost penniless. The barrel bottom was to be scraped dry just for the reckless plot of a penniless foreign adventurer. Why?

So was it really an untried and unproven scheme? That seems unlikely in view of the reversal of their most Catholic majesties.

Surely they had new intelligence that made them change their minds? But what was this new information?

Once again the dogs began to howl in the nearby jungle. Close by me a sleeping soldier awoke with a start and looked around. Quietly, I addressed him.

"Don't be afraid of the dogs. If they had any power you would be dead long ago. Every dog is bold on its own trash heap."

The startled young soldier heard little more than my reassuring tone of voice and went back to sleep.

Later, after some sleep, I joined my friend as he shared with me his thoughts as we patrolled the camp together.

What of the dreams of men? Dreams drive men to discover new lands, to write poetic epics, to build great empires. Dreams also inspire men to murder, to steal their neighbor's treasure, to make false charges and to lie away the lives of innocent others. Dreams, the vision of things unreal, can so haunt the spirit that the mind recreates the world to match the dream. Dreams can forewarn the body of imminent good or evil soon to come about. Is there a land of common vision whose dreamscape is shared by all men?

El Gringo is one of the great world masters of dreams. To El Gringo, his dream had been a white horse of the sea on which to ride the waves to victory.

Oh master of dreams, ships and mystery, why, why introduce savage Irish wolfhounds not only on the first voyage but on subsequent visits?

By all accounts the natives were peace-loving. Something was lying around at the back of the old attic that was the antiquarian's memory. If only he could regrasp that old idea, refind that lost scrap of knowledge . . .

Somewhere, in the back of my friend's mind, there was a hidden reason, an incongruity that begged for an explanation. The answer to this question was surely the answer to all the questions about the mysterious El Gringo. Dogs. Dogs. Dogs.

Yet El Gringo was many bad things but not a panicker or coward. Both my friend and I felt that the usual explanations of unnatural fear, overreaction and so on, on the part of El Gringo, almost explained it all but not quite.

As I remarked to my friend, "Almost - almost went over a cliff but almost didn't."

Yes, it was somehow about dogs. There was a mystery there all about liars and dogs and dogs and liars.

Just a few years previously, the man known as El Gringo, the man who was now the subject of the investigation - El Gringo - had praised the King and Queen of Castile, as sovereigns of the Isles of the Sea, an oddly limited but prophetic title for those who had usually been known as their most Catholic sovereigns. This title had been based on the strict theology that the whole world was destined to come under the dominion of the true Catholic faith.

It was at the royal court in Castile at the City of Sacred Faith that their most Catholic majesties had first met El Gringo, supposedly from Genoa, an independent state on the Mediterranean coast.

El Gringo, to all appearances a Catholic, had stated it to be his sacred duty to bring not only Christ but also the true Catholic Church to the new lands across the Ocean Sea, the Atlantic. Somehow these new lands were equated with India, an old land to the east. This apparently embraced the blasphemous and heretical view that the earth was round and that therefore the east could be approached from the west, a strange proposition for their most Catholic majesties to support.

Still, if the round earth theory should be proven somehow true, then wealth and power and profit should certainly come before erroneous if traditional teaching.

However this may be, El Gringo let it be known that he was fulfilling his chosen purpose in life, his destiny, in bringing to pass the words of the prophet Isaiah in chapter 66 of his book, verse 19.

"And I will send those who escape to Tarshish (Castile), Put and Lud, to Meshek, Rosh, Tubal and Javan, to the Isles afar off."

It was agreed between El Gringo and their most universal sovereigns that any new wealth gained from El Gringo's voyage of discovery was to be used to recover the Holy Land from the Mohammedan infidel and to place it again in Christian hands.

El Gringo was not only an eloquent speaker but also a religious man much given to fasting and prayer but his proposal for a new voyage of discovery was rejected by King Ferdinand and Queen Isabella. El Gringo left the City of Sacred Faith and began to make his way out of Castile towards the neighboring land of Oporto, hoping to get support there for his western adventure.

However, at this point and strangely, a high ranking cleric, one Angelo de Luisvilla, keeper of the monarch's purse, declared himself in favor of El Gringo's enterprise. Praising the plan for its small outlay and great potential, he offered to finance himself the proposed voyage of discovery if Ferdinand and Isabella did not wish to do so. From this point on everyone suddenly began to act as if the result of the voyage were a foregone conclusion.

Then, just as El Gringo was leaving Castile, a messenger rode a cloud of dust to summon the great stranger back to the court of Ferdinand and Isabella at the City of Sacred Faith.   His project was to be sponsored by their most universal sovereigns.   Truly an amazing even a miraculous reversal for their most Catholic majesties.

At this point, Bobadilla paused and I took the opportunity to put in my twopenceworth with some more old proverbs.

"It certainly is true," I nodded, "If it's worth taking, it's worth asking for. Audacity will receive its reward and Well begun is half finished."

My friend agreed with me and continued his thoughtful murmurings.

So . . the foreign upstart, fraud and liar then set sail with a small fleet of ships, navigated across the Atlantic and discovered the Isles of the West. Leaving the small port of Trees, El Gringo gave orders to sail in the name of Jesus, praying that Jesus and Mary be with him in the name of the holy trinity.

Obviously one to cover all bases both divine and terrestrial, he was promised 1/10 of all spoil and had also received from Ferdinand and Isabella, the titles of Admiral of the Atlantic, Viceroy, Governor General and Magistrate of all Monies. This was all remarkable for the leader of an expedition which was supposed to be based, in spiritual terms, at best on hope and, in worldly terms, on pure speculation.

Now, just a few years later this alien upstart was being charged with the maladministration of the isles he had discovered, theft, lies, unjustified murder of natives, slavery, hangings of noblemen - all of which could be summed up neatly as treason and blasphemy.

My friend the antiquarian and now as Bobadilla, the Castile royal representative charged with the investigation of El Gringo, looked at the first rays of the sun rising through the trees and jungle and listened to the sounds of one hundred birds and native creatures. Then the sound of foreign dogs began barking and howling in the distance.

It has often been said that a dog is

man's best friend. Maybe, but what does that tell us about the nature of man and what about the nature of dog?

All reports were adamant that most Indigenos were small, frail and non-aggressive. Again, like a refrain, my friend allowed the harsh barking to sink into his deeper mind. In its original paradisical state these islands knew only barkless, tame dogs and now savage wild animals from Ireland, Irish wolfhounds, were tearing apart men, women and children. The question was - Why?

*****

Chapter Five

The Court Pavilion

The royal investigator sets up a camp at which to gather evidence about the alleged crimes of El Gringo.

On the following morning the Castile investigators buried, with full benefit of clergy, their three fellow noblemen.

The mood of the mourners was solemn and puzzled and apprehensive. There were untold tales and threats and, somehow, strange spiritual forces at work here. As they looked around at the unusual forests and flora and absorbed the smells and airs of a new world, many wished in their hearts and souls to be back on the terra firma of Castile, a land much better known and loved by all.

"Cohen, my friend, this would be a good place for our headquarters, do you agree?"

"Of course, Bobadilla."

After the three corpses had been uneasily buried, the tents were erected in a circle and the layout of the camp took shape.

In the centre of the encampment, my friend set up our personal quarters of sleeping and living, somewhat to the south, with Primo's quarters to the east.

Lying between the living quarters was set out a tent-shaded court, a pavilion on poles for receiving subordinates and eventually, no doubt, for seating those subject to scrutiny and investigation - the dreaded duty of the entire encampment.

A large chair was set up for the royal investigator in front of a half circle of tables behind which were ranged around chairs for advisers. At each side of his throne was a space for bodyguards coming and going from the rear. At the front entrance to the pavilion there were permanent guards ranged on either side.

All in all, a neatly laid out primitive pavilion court was put together with the living quarters of the judges and inquisitors attached. Likewise, guards and lookouts surrounded the outer rim of the encampment. Able-bodied seamen with picks and shovels began to lay a road towards the center of the island. A road, mused my friend, the essence of empire. Where, really, would it lead?

My friend lost no time in outlining the investigative procedures to his right hand man, the hidalgo Primo along with Primo's assistants.

"We have a royal commission, an official written mandate to do what we are doing. Something is deeply wrong here. Evil, not good, rules. This should not be in a Christian empire.

"There is something deeply and subversively rotten about the whole new world enterprise. We have been asked to find out exactly what is wrong. We must not assume guilt in any particular aspect of our inquiries. Yet there must be something wrong, very wrong to call for a royal inquiry at this outpost of the empire.

"What we need to do is to find out what specifically is wrong and where and what and when and by whom precisely the undoubted abuses are taking place.

"It is not reasonably to be supposed that the good noble and Christian complainants are all liars but just why have so many things gone wrong here in New Castile which ought to be a model of Christian work among the heathen?

"For instance, we need to look at some strange, even weird, events on this island - any one of which could give rise to a capital charge against El Gringo."

Primo was clearly disturbed by this statement. My friend looked at Primo levelly and frankly.

"What's the matter, Primo?"

"Excellency, you are the royally appointed inquiring magistrate . . If the crimes are as serious as you say and I personally agree with you, Excellency, that El Gringo's crimes are enormous but then why should El Gringo not be summonsed here to answer for his atrocities?"

Just a flick of a smile crossed the face

of my friend.

"Yes, Primo, so that El Gringo can have an opportunity to admit avidly to all his capital offences. I agree but in view of the fact that El Gringo may be a denier of justice - even a liar - why give him a chance to deny all charges? Would it not be better to get some evidence, even specific detailed charges against El Gringo and then summon him to defend himself? I am asking you all to find such evidence and make just such specific charges. See?"

Primo brightened, "Great, for I have some such charges based on my expeditionary sailing experience with El Gringo."

"Then, Primo, try to find some answers, some reasons, some rationale, some evidence for the aberrations, the crimes, the perversions of justice, the selfishness that has taken over these unhappy islands under El Gringo. Let us have justice, reason, fairness and good explanations to set out the path to a civilized, law respecting investigation into life and justice and everyday business here in New Castile. What do you think my dear

Cohen?"

I agreed. "There is an old saying, You'll never know a man until you do business with him. So let us do business with El Gringo."

"Agreed, Excellency and Dr. Cohen, let us check him out and challenge him and see how much he respects law and order when it does not serve his theft and pride and lust and avarice . . And . . ." Primo searched for words, hopelessly.

"The gluttony and drunkenness and murders," suggested my friend with a straight face.

"Exactly, Excellency," Primo looked distinctly more cheerful, "and the specific charges at the moment are overtaxing, enslavement, skimming the cream, various hangings of noblemen who will not bow to him, cutting off of hands and feet, burning alive in hammocks, setting the dogs on innocent Indigenos."

"Primo, that last charge is a strange one, different from the others. It troubles me. It seems to be without reason. All the other charges are to punish, to discipline, to make conform, to make obedient with acts of cruelty."

"But really, Bobadilla, setting dogs on harmless men, that too is an act of cruelty," I suggested.

"Yes Cohen, but Indigenos are needed for work even in El Gringo's terms, slavery, so why drive them off when they are neither thieves nor attackers, when in fact they have not offended? They are a small, weak, evidently peaceable nativery. It's a strange move to drive away slaves and laborers."

I replied, "I have been thinking, perhaps El Gringo is merely establishing his authority, demanding respect, even fear or perhaps the dogs are merely to round up and to shepherd the slaves."

My friend considered for a moment then shook his head, "It seems that these Irish wolfhounds are being used to attack, savage and terrorize. However, we will keep an open mind . . ."

Bobadilla turned to the hidalgo.

"Primo, I would also ask you to investigate that allegation. Perhaps the allegation is untrue, unfounded. If it did happen, try to find out why. Talk to as many as you can, including the Indigenos.

"If El Gringo does set wild dogs on inoffensive natives, then perhaps he is insane, troubled with imaginary ghosts and ghouls and horrors. Perhaps his mind is one unfit to be a viceroy. On the other hand, if this charge is untrue, then maybe the other charges against him are false also."

Primo bowed out and left the camp with his bodyguard.

My friend stared thoughtfully after the departing group and began to ruminate aloud.

El Gringo is a unique enigma. As you have often reminded us, Cohen, Know the breed and know the dog but no one really knows the breed of the Admiral of the Atlantic. His background is clearly a cheap fabrication. He seems to have sprung out of the sea; the normal rules do not apply to this mysterious man but somehow dogs are a key to the mystery. There is an unanswered question there but I am not even sure of the question much less the answer. Yet to set dogs on peaceable natives for no apparent reason is strange.

Who but an Irishman would know about Irish wolfhounds? Is there some connection here to the Atlantic journeys of the Irish saints of long ago? Perhaps long forgotten sea chronicles, logs or maps?

*****

Chapter Six

El Gringo Refuses

The investigator, Bobadilla, accumulates considerable evidence against El Gringo and politely extends an invitation to the Governor.

Over the next few days the investigation makes good progress. A handwritten document sealed with the royal seal was sent by messenger to El Gringo. It included a copy of the antiquarian's authorization papers, the originals of which had been signed by the King and Queen.

El Gringo was requested to cooperate with the fully commissioned royal investigation which was being held into his conduct of the colony. The main charges were of corruption and brutality.

No answer was given by El Gringo, who did not recognize the court, either directly by word of mouth or indirectly by any relevant action taken. There was no flight into the jungle of a guilty man and no effort to contact the investigator and explain his innocence. Only a haughty contempt was the answer - clearly a refusal to cooperate, a play for time.

Meanwhile the evidence against El Gringo began to pile up like a trash heap.

Witnesses testified to El Gringo's ability to foretell the future, to manipulate and bind great monarchs. Witnesses were about equally divided as to whether this magic was the result of divine inspiration or of dark deals with Beelzebub. In either case the explanation was that El Gringo was a creature of the supernatural, destined to find a new world - a lucky deceiver.

At one point the antiquarian, Primo and I sat at the great table of judgment and talked about our findings so far.

Primo spoke up, "El Gringo is very very lucky he is not in jail."

"Truly it is said," I remarked sadly, "A lucky man needs only to be born."

"I agree," replied my friend. "But is El Gringo just lucky or is he well, yes, lucky but also sharp and shrewd and selfish and ruthless and murderous and manipulative; in short an arch-liar and fraud?

"His ability to foresee land before it appears - none of this makes sense in terms of normal reality. There is a missing link, an explanation that escapes me totally, something lying in the rubbishy old attic that is the scrapbook of my memories, something I can never seem to find, something that would solve it all."

"I truly believe," I answered, "that as you once said, magic is too simple an answer. It appears that El Gringo is inspired by either deity or the devil."

"My dear Cohen, magic is the same thing as dealing with Satan and I reject that as an explanation."

Then I pointed out, "Satan will deal with anyone and I truly suspect that Satan is El Gringo's master."

"In a manner of speaking that is quite possible," Bobadilla sighed. "Something is certainly wrong for it is a fact that floggings and hangings and arsons and limb cuttings of Christian Castile nobles must all give rise to a great hatred and a great reckoning. However, Satan is an unhelpful partner and the fact that El Gringo follows Satan does not in the least indicate that he receives any direct help or information from the evil one.

"I also refuse to believe that he receives direct guidance from God. If El Gringo were a saint, a paragon of Christian virtue perhaps the good one would guide him but we know what El Gringo is."

"But Excellency he is very fortunate." Primo interposed.

"Yes, but it follows that his good luck comes from some more earthly source not directly from God or the devil - not from the supernatural."

"Excellency," replied Primo solemnly, "I do not wish to contradict you but do I not have a duty to be honest and frank with your Excellency?"

"Most certainly Primo. That is why I

selected you as an honest and frank Christian man. Feel free."

"This man is charged with diabolical crimes and is guilty of overtaxing, skimming the extra taxes for himself, brutal and cruel murders and burnings and hangings."

The antiquarian smiled patiently and held up a gentle hand, "Suspected of - not guilty of."

"Agreed your Excellency but I have witnesses of good repute that he failed to make any effort to rescue half-dead whites from the slavery of the Indigenos and left them to languish in the hands of the savages. A small rescue party could have prevailed."

At this comment my friend perked up his ears, "Really. I have never heard of this. If the whites were Christians this is a capital charge that must be looked into. If Christians are in danger from hanging by their fellow Christians we have a duty, upon pain of death, to rescue them. Please investigate this one, Primo."

Then Primo bowed in satisfaction, "Of course, Senor."

"Who were these white men?"

Primo hesitated slightly for a moment and scrutinized the faces of those around him before replying, "Zombies, according to the information I have been given."

"Who on earth are zombies, Primo?"

"I have been told that they are half dead ones, your Excellency. I am not sure Excellency."

"Well, find out more about their ill-treatment and kidnapping."

Primo bowed but looked very uncomfortable at my friend and I for a moment, then brightened.

"Alas, Senors, I have been shown more hanged Castile noblemen and heard testimony of El Gringo enslaving not only Indigenos but also Castile Christian men - Christians, Excellency, dismembered and hanged without the benefit of clergy, Christians burnt alive and their gold stolen."

Primo paused for effect and indeed my friend listened sadly and shook his head in disapproval.

"Also Excellency, there is revolution in the air."

"You mean mutiny?"

"Just so, Senor. Mutiny."

"Of Castile or Indigeno?"

"Both, your Excellency. Both have said to me that they have had enough of this devil, this creature of Satan."

"Look Primo, my dear hidalgo, I need answers, not speculation, not guesses, not superstitions and not 'possible vague conclusions' - hard facts, reality, cruel but true answers and explanations."

"I understand your Excellency but there is evidence, hard fact, reality that points, can point, only to unseen powers being at work here. The only unseen powers are those of good or evil. Yes, there seems to be evidence of these forces at work."

"Such as . . ?"

"Very good Senor, I will tell you. How did El Gringo know that he was sailing to a group of islands unless he had the devil's help and information? He was to convert India not an unknown group of isles to Roman Catholicism. So why did he sail west and know that he was headed for islands not the landmass of India? How did he know when they would hit land and tell me as the watchman accordingly unless the devil told him in advance? Yet I know that magic is not a good enough answer to bring out all the truths."

Just at that moment, my friend closed his eyes thoughtfully.

"I do not know the answer to your questions, my dear hidalgo, but I do know one thing - it is high time that we began to find some answers. Send for the foreigner, arrest him if necessary in the name of my authority from their most Catholic majesties. Bring him here, preferably without force, but bring him, understand?"

"Of course, Excellency, but I will need a larger company of soldiers."

The antiquarian nodded briskly and saluted as his hidalgo bowed out respectfully and with some enthusiasm to accomplish his task. For the hidalgo, Primo, long since cheated by El Gringo, this was going to be a pleasure . . .

*****

Chapter Seven

El Gringo Appears

El Gringo is arrested and brought face to face with his investigators. Accused of his crimes, he is clamped in chains as he is forced to submit.

In a few hours Bobadilla, the royal investigator, was back in his chair as the head of the pavilion court. An impressive, even noble figure stood before him surrounded by the Castile soldiers of the royal inquiry. The prisoner was tall, sturdy and broad-shouldered, hawk-nosed and ruddy-faced with sharp blue eyes.

He spoke defiantly, "I demand to know by what authority you bring me, the Governor of New Castile, here as a prisoner."

"By the authority of their most Catholic majesties," replied my friend.

"I demand to see your original charter, not copies or fakes, the true papers of investigation from Old Castile, if you have any original."

Bobadilla nodded, "I am a royal appointed investigator from the Royal Court of the Sacred Faith of Castile and these are my papers of authorization to carry out an inquiry into your conduct here as Governor."

The papers from the King and Queen were passed over to the prisoner. Signed, sealed and now delivered, quoted my friend to himself with satisfaction.

El Gringo read and studied the papers slowly and thoroughly. He was obviously stunned and then he handed them back to my friend, in silence.

Bobadilla took advantage of the brief interlude to glance sideways and assess his prisoner. Here was a foreigner of unknown and strange origin and his supposed Genoan origin was clearly a lie.

Before we had embarked from Castile,

Bobadilla had had his spies inspect the Colum family records in Genoa - there was no trace of any Christopher at any time that could refer to the birth of this mid-aged mariner.

Yet, my friend could not but be impressed.

Here stood a great man of leadership, dignity, courage and natural nobility but a man of honesty, integrity, humanity and generosity? Perhaps not.

Of course one or two Genoans might look like this but not many. Here was a man from the north of Europe rather than a southerner. He was tall, red-haired, ruddy skinned, blue-eyed, hook-nosed - truly a man of great foresight and power. But who was he and where was he really from? Why did he hide his origins? Because of a great crime? Who or what were his brothers?

My friend the antiquarian pondered these questions.

Brothers, ah yes, of course, brothers indeed. As for his brothers, how could or why should one accept them as such? If he himself was not on the records of the clan of which he claimed membership, why should his so-called brothers be accepted as such? If he was a liar, a mystery in his origins, why should not his brothers also be impersonators? Companions, part of the overall fraud of El Gringo, certainly in this sense members of the clan yes. But brothers - who knows? There is only El Gringo's word for it and that we know to be highly questionable.

It is always impressive and even intimidating to be a member of a powerful family so much so that rogues often pretend to have relatives - kill me and my family will ask questions they seem to say - a sure ploy of many a solitary but cunning deceiver.

El Gringo was clearly struck dumb with shock.

The investigator took advantage of the short, sharp silence to make his point, a not dissimilar one to the speech he had made to Primo, comforting him for his lack of nobility. Truly, sauce for the goose is sauce for the gander.

"Governor, Admiral El Gringo, you seem to be surprised, sir."

El Gringo gasped, took a deep breath, looked far into the future skies and spoke from his soul, "Yes sir, I am greatly troubled . . ."

"You should know, Admiral - that no one, however eminent or powerful, is above the law - that is, of course, no one but their majesties."

El Gringo went pale as his body shook. Then he staggered and clutched his staff.

*****

Chapter Eight
Chained

The investigator formally charges El Gringo with stealing gold, tax evasion, murder and other serious crimes.

My friend, the antiquarian addressed El Gringo, respectfully.

"Governor of New Castile, please be seated, your Excellency."

"I prefer to stand."

"Very well. Just as you wish."

"We have summoned you here by the authority of their most Catholic majesties, Ferdinand and Isabella of Castile, to answer the following charges. After I have read out the charges you may respond. During or after any such response I may choose to further question you about these charges. Do you understand?"

El Gringo nodded slightly and coldly.

Glancing briefly at his papers which he continually shuffled and reshuffled and laid out in front of him, my friend intoned the charges with a sigh, shaking his head sadly.

"You may well be innocent of all these charges. Many a good man has been so accused out of envy and we will certainly give you every chance to find witnesses and evidence and prove your innocence . . .

"However, it has been charged on good and responsible witness that despite setting sail to these islands in the name of Jesus and Mary, and discovering a new world and naming your headquarters Holy Master, that is to say Christ, and despite having the responsibility of a Christian governor, you have instituted cruel and barbarous punishments for those who opposed you.

"You have enslaved both Indigeno and white men and created such chaos that large numbers have rebelled. You have overtaxed the settlers, failed to pay wages due, set savage dogs to drive away the Indigenos despite the fact that they are a small, weak and peaceable people . . ."

At this point, my friend scrutinized the great foreigner closely, searching El Gringo's eyes for any hint or clue. The governor made no response and gazed bleakly and coldly into the distance.

"You are accused of failing to keep any books of account and of stealing gold and dividing it among your cronies and your own family and paying no royal tax thereon.

"You have also hanged true born noblemen of Castile, of whom you are not one. You and your brothers are mere foreign upstarts. By the way, your brothers have been arrested and are being held as your accessories.

"There is also a very serious charge, very well proven by numerous witnesses of good repute that you failed to rescue white hostages who had been seized by the Indigenos."

It was now El Gringo's turn to look puzzled.

"There was no such incident . . ." he

began, then paused reflecting.

"Half-dead white men left to perish? Does that shake your memory?"

El Gringo paled but soon recovered with a savage glare.

My friend remembered the old saying that the best means of defense is attack and braced himself.

He was not caught unawares when El Gringo pointed a long finger and cried.

"What real power do you have over me to so convict me? Your charter says only to investigate charges. You have no right to convict me. I demand to be sent home to my only earthly masters, Ferdinand and Isabella, their most Catholic majesties."

"Not yet. No. No. No, not quite yet Governor, my investigations are not complete. As for my powers, I have absolute power over you otherwise I would not have had you arrested."

At this point I could not help adding my twopenceworth. "If a dog cannot bite, it should not show its teeth."

My friend nodded to me and continued to address the Governor. "Once again I must remind you that it was you who brought barking, savage dogs to this paradise on your first voyage. Why? What was your original reasoning? It's not a recognized means of warfare."

"I demand to be returned to Castile to my only masters. I have closely scrutinized your charter. Your remit is to investigate and then report back to the King and Queen."

"I have no intention of so reporting until I have made a thorough and just investigation," responded my friend. "My orders to you now are to go and set free all your prisoners - those native or white whom you are setting up - no doubt - to be hanged. These proposed hangings are not for murder, grand theft or for treason. Therefore, the charges are illegal and the prisoners must be released.

"Do you understand, Admiral of the Atlantic? By the way, when you first set out, why were you not given the title of Admiral of the Indian Ocean? Weren't you supposed to be sailing to the Indian Ocean to convert India to Christ? The Church still teaches that the earth is flat, so why sail to the west to find India to the east? Have the King and Queen come to believe that the earth is a globe?

"And what is all this business about a new world? Surely, India is an old, old, well known continent, not a newly discovered one? And why is your name not on the records of the Genoan family that you claim as your own?"

"I refuse to recognize the validity of this court. Your investigation and a duty for you to report back to King Ferdinand and Queen Isabella is not in question. What I dispute is your right to demand answers from me and to judge me - that is, I deny your right to conduct a court as opposed to an inquiry."

"That is an interesting theoretical point, Admiral and Governor, but I do have a clear right to conduct an inquiry and take all action necessary to facilitate justice and truth. That includes ordering you to snap your so-called brothers into line with the law."

"They cannot so act when under arrest."

The antiquarian at last began to show

slight signs of anger and disgust. "Not all your lackeys have been arrested. Your assistants, relatives or otherwise, will begin to obey the laws of Castile. Is that clear?"

El Gringo stared back like a stone idol at the Castile investigator.

Primo stood up respectfully. "With the courts permission . . ."

My friend had no intention of losing the initiative and waved him back into his seat.

"Primo I will put your point to the Governor so that it will be presented impartially."

Primo bowed respectfully.

Then turning to El Gringo, my friend continued.

"But you Governor, it comes into my head to ask you why, if you are the Christian man of integrity you claim to be, why did you rob a poor sailor of the promised prize of nobility to the one who first saw land? When the watch cried out *land* you came on deck and took control, steering the ship and claiming to have been the first to see land. This was an act of pure blasphemy, perverting the solemn oath of their most Catholic majesties and falsely claiming the prize of nobility for yourself and all your heirs and successors forever. What have you to say?"

Primo, overcome with tears, began to speak, pointing a finger at the foreigner.

"Through you, Governor, I have lost my faith in God."

"Please, Primo, control yourself. It was not God but man, this man, who stole nobility from you. Truly God gets the blame for so many of man's vilest deeds of hatred and greed.

"And again, Admiral, it has been reported also on good evidence that you had the greatest confidence in the outcome of your unique voyage of discovery. How did you know in advance what you were going to find? Islands instead of the Indian continent? And how were you able to warn the watchman when and where he was to look for land? Magic? Divine revelation?"

"You may think so, if you so wish," replied the Governor.

The antiquarian nodded shrewdly at the great discoverer. "Yes, wouldn't you like us all here to believe that. But you will be disappointed to discover that we do not so believe, neither I nor any of my fellow inquirers. Do we my friends?"

Neither Primo nor any of the other Castile gentlemen ranged around felt that this was a good time to argue with their leader. Evidently overcoming some degree of doubt and puzzlement they dutifully smiled and murmured their agreement with my friend.

No, of course they did not believe that El Gringo was a magician or divinely inspired. Not in the least. How silly, Excellency. They shuffled uneasily.

"Then we must try to find another explanation, mustn't we, Governor?" added my friend.

"Like what?"

"Like something in your previous hidden life for instance. O yes, well hidden by your many changes of name. For example your life in the great capitals and seaports. Whom did you previously sail under?"

"Are you here to investigate my previous life or my work here on New

Castile?"

"Both Admiral. One thing leads to another. Surely you understand that background often explains later conduct.

Here I interjected once more with some satisfaction. "As we say in Castile - Long runs the fox that is not caught at last."

My friend continued, "I understand that you personally are to receive ten percent of all the spoils found here?"

El Gringo nodded.

The antiquarian shook his head, incredulously. "You, a penniless foreigner, to undertake a voyage that anyone of ten thousand Castile nobles or gentlemen could have undertaken with equal success? And to get ten percent of all spoils. Astonishing.

"Yes, Governor, I am about to grant you your request. I will indeed send you back to their most Catholic majesties to be judged by them. Until the outcome of that trial is known, I must take control of the Governor's house, hoards, function and documents as evidence.

"This is, of course, purely in my

capacity as a trustee, a custodian until your case has been adjudicated and either you have been cleared and reinstated as Governor or until a new Governor has been appointed. I have no personal interests in your estates, Governor, you may be assured. This is entirely a matter for their majesties.

"To prevent your escape, I must of course ask you to submit to enshacklement as a prisoner of their majesties. You will set sail at once."

My friend raised his eyebrows in an unspoken query.

The great discoverer, now a mere criminal, lifted up his head proudly and replied with dignity.

"I understand. I look forward to revisiting my earthly sovereigns in a few weeks time."

Stretching out his hands and planting his feet apart to receive the chains, the sailor of mystery, the master of many seas was clothed in shackles and led away.

*****

Chapter Nine

An Admiral in Castile

El Gringo is taken back in chains to the King and Queen in Castile to face charges of treason, tax stealing, taking bribes, whipping the innocent, wrongful hangings and burning his foes alive.

In the treeful and jungled Isles of the West, the Land of Youth in ancient Gaelic legend, many beautiful and peaceful ships sailed in and billowed out among the warm lagoons to and from Old Castile and indeed many other countries.

At times pleasant breezes blew. Of course, at other times the Atlantic was a fierce mountainous valley of green sea-weeded hills but then so what? Some men were destined to sail and some were destined to sink. So why worry?

Faced with the uncontrolled elements of wind and sea and cold and rain and ice, seamen are often fatalistic. Every ship, whether coming in or going out had its own unique messages even superstitions. It is not difficult to see how superstitions can slowly build up.

The sea has many supernatural elements and sometimes they do, undoubtedly, form a long-term pattern so that repeated strange sequences become awed beliefs or superstitions, facts of faith and fear without rational explanation. Such a belief in the Isles was the myth of the zombie recurring time and again from witnesses of good repute.

That is why seamen are superstitious. They have seen it all happen so many times without any scientific reason.

Numbers and systems of numbers in the universe are at work far beyond the ken of man and the numbered work of the stars are downright needed to sail a ship. Numbers and number paradigms from exemplars of the great unknown form the archetypes and subtle designs of luck. And luck added to luck leads on to loved or dreaded destiny.

Perhaps it was the destiny of El Gringo to succeed in his adventures; perhaps he was thrown out from the seas of history a courageous sailor, lucky but out of his depth as a leader.

As the antiquarian often quoted - Some men are like fire - a good servant but a bad master.

El Gringo was a burning masthead out of control.

However, not only luck and destiny came from the tall ships that visited the multi-green bird-song Isles of New Castile. Solid, down to earth news of real events in the world came and went, sometimes with little embellishment or exaggeration. After all, a death is a death and a verdict is either guilty or not guilty, a birth is either a son or daughter and similar events leave little to color or to paint in misty scenes. Mere adjectives, true or false, do little to disguise such basic facts of life.

So it was that over the next few

months Primo and his associates built up a series of accounts on the fate of El Gringo as he had fared back in the courts of Old Castile and these reports were duly presented to the royal investigator, Bobadilla. Eventually, of course, official word would come to the investigator but the workings of officialdom were slow and painful and ambiguous and convoluted.

In the meantime, it seemed that, from fragmented reports, some real and decisive events had taken place . . .

El Gringo and his brothers, it was said, had reached the shores of Old Castile on 20 November, 1500. The governor's jailor was the Hidalgo Alfonso who had offered, out of respect for the sailor, to set El Gringo free from his chains but the famous explorer refused, saying that it was the law of their most Catholic majesties Isabella and Ferdinand that all major prisoners should be shackled. In this way the Admiral made sure that he would be pitied and thus receive sympathy, at least from the ladies of the court of Castile.

Of course, as Primo pointed out when the news reached Bobadilla, the ladies included the Queen herself.

Still in chains, El Gringo was taken to Sacred Faith, capitol of Castile and lodged in a Carthusian Monastery at which time he had stated, "My body is here, my heart in the New World."

"Primo, our present charges against El Gringo may not be the last word. Who knows? He is such a good liar that he may talk his way out of these just charges, just as he talked his way into the incredible deal in the first place. Let us continue to investigate the Admiral so that we will have something to fall back on if he lies his way out of his present predicament."

"Absolutely Excellency, he is the great manipulator. I would not put anything past him. And each day I am checking out his further malfeasances with Indigenos, the Christian Castile and also with the Negro slaves from Africa. I am building up an even more horrifying picture of his crimes than we ever suspected. Perhaps we should have held on to him longer?"

"No, Primo," I pointed out to the hidalgo, "he had a right as a Royal Governor to appear before their majesties, just as St. Paul had a right to appear before Caesar. What we are engaged in now is our second line of offence in case he should ever escape or finish out his sentence. Carry on with the good work - little by little the way the cat ate the fish."

"Yes Dr. Cohen, one day we will unravel the whole mystery of the great liar and fraud."

As Primo and I continued our investigations during the days and weeks that followed, a fuller account of events back in Old Castile began to sail in from the great ships that visited the New World. These were the mariners who went to sea to trade for foods such as corn, potatoes, tomatoes, avocados or for pleasures such as tobacco or the song-birds or for the lifelong security promised by gold and silver. For gold and silver do not rot like food nor die like song-birds nor do they go up in smoke like tobacco. As I once reflected to my friend, the antiquarian:

The wise man will hold
Silver and gold

Yes, there was a lot to attract ships from all over Christendom to the idyllic

Isles of New Castile.

Bobadilla continued to rely for information on Primo who, in turn, presided over a large network of informants covering both the incoming seamen and rumors that now and again wafted gently over the Isles of the Blest.

It is a fact that El Gringo was entrusted to the custody of his secret supporter, Don Gastoni, a Franciscan friar from Caves Monastery in Sacred Faith. At this monastery the Admiral, certainly now no longer Governor, wrote to a lady love of his, who is a lady-in-waiting to Queen Isabella.

What exactly did he claim to be his justification for his excesses and greeds and thefts and murders?

It seems that he let it be known subtly and sinuously that his brothers, who were also his lieutenants, tended to be either a little on the weak side in the case of Jacob or a little on the harsh side in the case of Varth. So it was left to El Gringo to take firm control.

His other main supporters and assistants engaged in theft and were mutinous.   Other lower down settlers would not work an inch of ground but rather lay back in hammocks and watched the growth of valuable native plants such as tomato, tobacco and corn.

So calm and healthy and free-breathing were these Isles of Youth that the settlers would work only if compelled to do so by vicious brute force and flagellation.

It was a case of mutiny, followed by lying back in hammocks and doing nothing to repay their most Catholic majesties. Only whippings and burnings and, in extreme cases, hangings, could sufficiently encourage the others, so to speak, to get out of bed and do some work to repay the outlay spent by the Castile government.

Finally, El Gringo suggested that in order to protect trades and profits and create safe sea places in which to travel it was incumbent upon him as an admiral to do whatever, however extreme, whenever, whyever, wherever he could to create and preserve the Queen's peace in the long waterways of the New World.

In the meantime, before El Gringo's

trial, a formal list of the investigator's specific charges took the form of seven indictments against El Gringo, written up by Bobadilla. These were sent back to Castile with good witnessed attestations.

Formally the major charges were against three brothers - El Gringo and his alleged two brothers Jacob and Varth, as follows:

1. Drove hard and deprived the Castile troops and brutally punished them and half starved them.
2. Waged unjust war against the Indigenos.
3. Set dogs on Indigenos and drove them off for no reason.
4. Enslaved Indigenos until they died like flies from hard work.
5. Did not allow Indigenos to be baptized so as to sell them as slaves.
6. Made secret hoards of pearls and gold, stolen from the Crown.
7. Hangings, burnings alive and tortures of Christian Castile, including noblemen.

The question of right or wrong, innocent or guilty, hangs over the whole of this story.

El Gringo, was he a good man or a

bad man? We must see him as good or bad - he has no middle persona. He must be right or wrong.

It is the same thing with an empire. A civilization can become great, an empire can be built on lies and hate and murder and stupidity if the empire builders are fierce enough and vile enough and bloody enough. But can such an empire last for long?

Well . . great empires that last are built on highways and law and order and free markets and entrepreneurship and local autonomy and the swift expulsion of foreign invaders. A common language is vital.

Yet the road, the simple road is always the key to empire, the humble peasant road upon which common persons can walk.

The Castile Empire was truly a branch of the ancient Roman Empire - one of many such branches. The main help that it brought to the new world was supposedly law and order and food, farming and trade and business and exchanges and jobs and incomes and wealth but could all those good things be brought about on the basis of lies and bribery and greed and corruption and theft?

Well, let us think about that . . . A clean fountain gives out clean water and out of a dirty well you can bring out only filthy water. Is this true? All right. Let us observe and see. Is it in the nature of empires to do good? If the people in an empire get education and a living and a home and food and health and happiness and language and justice from it, can it be wrong?

When the rule of the local tyrants and beheaders and robbers brings only dyslexia, poverty and sickness, misery, confusion, ignorance and helplessness beneath the dictators power, how is this independence and freedom, as some would label it?

Is it all right for a bully, a tyrant, a torturer, rapist, a mass murderer, a liar, a thief, to steal and to kill and to destroy just because he is of the same skin-color and background? But if he is not of the same creed or complexion or tongue, then he becomes a fiend, an exploiter, a foreign imperialist.

These and similar questions were discussed at the meetings of the Castile ruling council where the charges against the Governor were debated. Of the elders who made up the communal council, about one half were on one side and about one half were on the other side. Some said that a tyrant was a tyrant and whatever his color or creed should nevertheless be sent away. Yet others held that only if the tyrant was a foreigner should he be deposed. Kill the foreigner.

Is empire therefore the future of humanity? Is it inevitable that mankind should all join hand in each other's hand to form a new great world order that will live forever? If not, will narrow selfish fears and greeds help all the earth to join together and live?

*****

Chapter Ten

Judgment in Castile

The King and Queen ignore the huge evidence against El Gringo.

Just as he had hinted in his letter to Johanna, a lady-in-waiting to the Queen, El Gringo's self-justification to the Castile court was that a lawless and quite new, an unprecedented situation with mutinies and rebellion, called for tough, crude measures.

The colonists, he claimed, wanted to eat locusts and lie around, not to work or to repay the investments of Ferdinand and Isabella and their supporters.

The wholesale slaughter of Indigenos, who were largely unarmed and apparently peaceful, still remained an unaddressed mystery.

El Gringo also claimed to have seen visions and heard voices. Later he also claimed to have seen a vision of the death of Bobadilla which did not bother the royal investigator, not at all.

After all, as the antiquarian often pointed out, all men die sometime. So what?

From prison El Gringo would also ask, What if the Isles had not been producing wealth and had suffered from a bad climate? Did this justify a Viceroy being enchained? Indeed, even some of El Gringo's former enemies and the returned disgruntled colonists were appalled. Such harsh treatment of a high ranking potentate made for many uneasy sleeps among the nobility.

Isabella and Ferdinand were shocked at the strong self defense of their Viceroy. In his letter to the Queen's lady-in-waiting, the Governor had claimed some biblical justification. El Gringo claimed that he had been divinely guided to discover these new worlds.

Perhaps the words of Isaiah referring to ships of Castile were coming true.

Perhaps some vague ideas of Revelation were being fulfilled. Also, the Viceroy claimed to be inspired by the letters of the Apostles to preach the word to the world since God had made him the messenger of a new heaven and a new earth.

Just as in his letter to the Queen's lady-in-waiting, Donna Johanna, El Gringo pleaded to the court that it was a new thing that a man like Bobadilla, sent out to hold an enquiry, should collect traitors and rebels and call them as witnesses against the Governor who had had to rule over them.

This royal investigator had taken over El Gringo's house, gold, servants, goods and papers and had hidden and withheld those papers that the Viceroy needed for his defense. What an unjust judge. But God, our Lord, abides in his power and wisdom and will punish the ungrateful.

In addition, El Gringo kept the chains on his hands and feet until their most Catholic majesties would command them to be removed. Even then, the Admiral swore that he would preserve the chains as memories of the scant recompense he received for his services. The Admiral had discovered the New World and received iron fetters and shackles in return. If perversely he had stolen the New World and given it to Africa, Castile could not have shown him greater enmity.

This raises a very sinister question. When he heard of this argument by El Gringo, the royal investigator asked the question: Just how does one steal a continent and give it to usurpers? El Gringo, more than anyone, should have known the answer to that puzzle.

At any rate, while discovering new lands and mountains of gold for the King and Queen, El Gringo had founded an earthly paradise only for his very own planters to mutiny against him.

El Gringo also pointed out that a man had been sent out to judge him, namely Bobadilla, who knew very well that he had only to lie and slander in order to take over the Governor's status, gold, house and papers. This, of course, was completely untrue and unfair to Bobadilla who was acting in the role of an impartial investigator and trustee of assets.

El Gringo further made the false charge that Bobadilla, it was further alleged, had also embezzled gold that the Admiral had hoarded secretly to protect it for safe delivery to their most Catholic majesties. El Gringo also pointed out that he was being treated like a general who had mishandled a campaign. Yet the natives of New Castile had been scattered all over the forests and jungles.

There had been no Indigeno army to defeat and where there were no towns or treaties or roads there could be no real law and order. In short, the New World had been chaos to which he was bringing order.

The Governor referred to the royal investigator's accusations that he, El Gringo, had set free criminals and bribed colonists but in this respect, the Governor alleged that the investigator had obtained complaints from low-class rabble against a Viceroy of the Realm.

Bobadilla had been supposed to be an impartial enquirer into El Gringo's conduct. Yet if he were to find the Governor and Admiral at fault, the same inquisitor was to take over as Viceroy.

Surely here was a grave conflict of interest.

Of course, neither the antiquarian nor I had any interest in El Gringo's position or his gold. Of course, in reality, Bobadilla was to take over only on a temporary basis and all final allocations of wealth or power were to be at the sole discretion of the King and Queen.

Yet, El Gringo's final plea was, Do not judge me as the Governor of a law abiding city but as a sea captain who was to conquer a numerous and war-like nation, persons of no fixed abode either in highlands or in jungles and of strange and many different customs and beliefs.

All in all, El Gringo made out such a case for himself with his lies, false accusations and his insidious self-justifications that Isabella and Ferdinand agreed to support their former Viceroy.

A last tragic scene was hypocritically playacted out by El Gringo as he, the Great Explorer, held up his chains in mute protest.

Eventually, El Gringo was recalled to court, had his chains removed, was treated with honor and re-recognized as Admiral of the Atlantic, thus being restored to all his full royal rights and privileges, Governor of the New World, Viceroy of their most Catholic majesties and so on and so on.

The investigator, Bobadilla, was to be suspended and in his place a new investigatory commissioner was to be appointed to New Castile. All the royal investigator's acts were cancelled.

Queen Isabella and King Ferdinand apologized to El Gringo, humbly claiming that they had been misunderstood. El Gringo's arrest and imprisonment had been against their royal knowledge and consent. How could they refuse a sailor who had justified a divine mission and who had meekly asked pardon for his excesses and errors?

Finally, their most Catholic majesties also sent El Gringo a million golden pieces in compensation.

Surely El Gringo seemed to hold more than mortal sway over the King and Queen. Or as the investigator had asked, Did he simply know too much? El Gringo saw his discovery as the greatest deed that ever mortal man had achieved and evidently their most Catholic majesties were in agreement.

Word soon reached Bobadilla that El Gringo had been set free and was expected soon to return to New Castile.

The royal investigator called together his court of inquiry and announced that El Gringo had been authorized to take back all that Bobadilla had been holding in trust. The question on everyone's lips was, Why? Why? The investigator spoke one last line to his pavilion court.

"I, Francesco Bobadilla, declare that I do not believe in magic. Any truly Christian believer and scientific enquirer is surely prompted, rather than resorting to superstition, to ask rational questions like, What does El Gringo know that gives him such power over the King and Queen? What does he know that so many bright and high-born clerics and nobles attribute his power directly to God or the devil?

"Furthermore I, Francisco Bobadilla, do not accept these explanations. I simply ask, Why should the powers of good or evil so consistently leap and jump to the help of a person of such selfish, deceitful, brutal and self-serving greed?"

*****

Chapter Eleven
Deals and Conspiracies

Before the imminent return of the Governor to New Castile, the royal investigator sets out to discover if there are any more uncovered facts about El Gringo which might explain his strange power over the King and Queen.

The pavilion court came together one last time to assess the news of the granting of freedom and the reinstatement of El Gringo and the expected soon return to New Castile of the Admiral, Governor and Viceroy.

The antiquarian addressed me and his fellow investigators and in particular the hidalgo Primo.

"There is one charge that we have not proven against El Gringo. Of course he has been cleared of everything by their most Catholic majesties, yet we did not officially mention his failure to rescue the Castile white captives who had been held by the Indigenos. This is so well attested to that we need to have the charge on the record before we bow out and resign the isles to their former tyrant.

"Perhaps the relatives of those so abandoned by the Admiral will include some powerful nobles who can exact a price for the loss of their kindred. We put this charge to the one side because for some reason you have never been able to fully answer my queries on the matter. We must leave it as our just legacy to the great foreigner and liar . . . What exactly is the problem?"

The group of investigators had begun to look sheepish and embarrassed. They looked at Primo somewhat guiltily and then he spoke up with the brave air of a reluctant martyr.

"Oh yes Excellency, we have all investigated the case of the white zombies but the only information we can get is steeped in superstition and alleged magic and we all well know and agree with, absolutely agree with, your Excellency's position that magic is not a good or rational or scientific or even a Christian explanation of things that we do not understand. So," he added lamely, "we have had little to say to your Excellency about that matter of white zombies."

"Zombies being a native word for hostage . . ?"

"No, Excellency, with all due respect to you, it means a creature who is neither living nor dead, but an in-between returner from the dead, one who is controlled by a Voodoo zombie master."

At this point Primo had begun to finger a rosary with great intensity.

Bobadilla shook his head in disbelief then calmly his eyes focused into the far distance. Then in a very relaxed tone he addressed the court.

"I begin to see where the problem lies. I have been too scathing of magic and the supernatural such that I have scared off your genuine and honest and decent reports. It is my fault. Please forgive me, my dear friends and colleagues. We are all going into the mists of winter snows and El Gringo is sailing back into the sunny harbors of green sea-weeded life and light. It behooves us to help and not to suspect or reject each other. Please be free to tell me all that you have found out."

At this point I stepped forward and addressed my friend the antiquarian and the others.

"I also have been a student of folklore and superstition and folk wisdom for over 40 years since I was a youth and I have never heard the word zombie - except here. Furthermore, Primo, tell me in words of one syllable, in very simple terms, what precisely is a zombie?"

"We will check it out thoroughly, Dr. Cohen, so as to give your Excellency a good and measured answer."

Then Primo addressed Bobadilla and bowed slightly.

"Yes, it does concern magic but really Excellency, really and truly, the magic is no belief of ours. It is entirely a perception of the Indigenos." Then he addressed the other investigators. "Is not that the case colleagues?"

The rest of the court team agreed in a somewhat relieved way as they looked at each other for confirmation and nodded their approval.

"Yes, your Excellency we will make a big effort to find out more about this."

"Above all, try to find out the family names of those so abandoned by El Gringo."

The company nodded uncomfortably and rather awkwardly, Primo brought closure to this phase of the proceedings with the phrase, "Until we know more."

The entire assembly, including my friend the antiquarian, nodded to each other in agreement.

"There is no hurry," Bobadilla smiled, "Let us find out the answers slowly, painstakingly even insidiously."

I added with a smile, "Do it little by little, the way the cat ate the fish."

"Well, to move on to other points," said my friend, "I am even more suspicious of El Gringo now that he has been, from all accounts, set free to return here as Viceroy to continue his malfeasances.

"So Ferdinand and Isabella ask me to investigate him and when I do so and try to stop his thefts and murders and excesses in the only legal way I can - then they reverse me."

"It's clear," I spoke up stoutly in support of my friend, "that El Gringo knows too much about Ferdinand and Isabella so that their conscience goes one way and their greed another. Theirs cannot be a rational verdict, only a verdict based on inside dealings. The agreement was that the Admiral was to get 1/10 of all spoils but he was ripping off 1/3 from all and sundry and therefore stealing from the crown.

"Why did Ferdinand and Isabella not resent this, detest it and punish it? Ferdinand and Isabella paid for El Gringo's whole adventures. It is said that whoever pays the piper, calls the tune. Why did Ferdinand and Isabella not call a halt to this tune of lies and murder and enslavement and torture and even direct theft from their majesties themselves?"

Bobadilla looked down the long road

that led from the camp, a road that had never been there before the coming of the Castile. Then he wondered aloud, Where would that road lead? What would be the future for this road now that the tyrant was to come back? Where would he, the investigator, go? To some distant lotus eater's isle?

Primo replied quietly. What of the people of the Isles? Would their wealth, their fruit and fish and rich green jungles all be scraped bare? Would their peoples, the Indigenos, be fleeced and slaughtered like sheep? Who or what are these sailors and traders? Christians or robbers in the name of Christ? God, in the name of God, they lie and cheat. God, in the name of God, they murder and thieve.

Primo lowered his eyes from the long road, to the stance of road beneath his feet and asked rhetorically. What of this road of empire? Surely, it was meant to be a path of peace for the feet of those who brought good news? Good news of Jesus savior of the world, good news of one who saved from sin and death. Not a safe path for those who seize and slaughter. That

would be the true judgment of the road.
Would the road of empire be a road of law,
a road of safety for the poor and hungry?
Or a road of riches for red-handed robbers,
a road of blood and arrogance and pride?
And what of the church, where would it
stand with empire? For the rich or for the
poor, what kind of law? Could one mere
man forgive another man for all his sins -
let men forgive each other and put God out
of business, sorry God but we don't need
your help - we are too rich.

So where does the road of empire
really lead? If it leads to the temple of
justice that is all we need for truth is Christ
and truth is all we need.

So why has the church supported
such crimes and why did it encourage
Ferdinand and Isabella to fund the original
voyage of discovery? Since when is the
church a speculator in long querulous
voyages of discovery.

What is the point in trying to be a fair
and impartial investigator in this crooked
world where even the highest lay or cleric
are motivated by hidden deals or
conspiracies? Better to be a monk - a

hermit living in a cave - praying through life to eternity on a rock of abstinence, abstinence from the two vilest and most corrupt influences of all - man and woman. Yet Ferdinand and Isabella are not one whit worse than the rest, only more powerful.

Although Primo's perspective was different from that of my friend and I, for after all we were interlopers in time and from a faraway place, we listened with respect to his thoughtful questions.

*****

Chapter Twelve

What are Zombies?

Part of Bobadilla's new investigation of El Gringo is now focused on what part Zombies might have played in the Governor's brutalities.

After this disgruntled, misanthropic speech, which was no more than a reflection of the entire court's disgust at the inexplicable setting free and the reinstatement of El Gringo, the royal investigator dismissed the meeting.

Over the next few days Bobadilla made discreet inquiries about the zombie and set out to master a general picture of the belief.

Soon my friend was hunting through his collection of folk wisdom, tales and superstitions and shaking his head in amazement.

"Beliefs and Superstition of the Peasantry of Here, There and Thither" would have been a good collective title for his library and this prized collection was written and published by a diversely qualified body of scholars, diarists, philosophers, travelers and raconteurs from many nations.

It was clear that ghosts were almost universally believed in. Trolls or gnomes and berserkers or metamorphists lived in many different Nordic lands, green vegetable giants in much of western Christendom, merry mermaids sang on all the seven seas, the banshee wailed and foretold of a soon coming death in the dark misty hills of Ireland and all the other isles off the western coast of Scotland.

Vampires, the undead who, to stay alive, suck the blood of the living in many different cultures of eastern Christendom, Romania, Russia, Hungary and other places.

Werewolves or men who mutate into wild dogs in England, France, Spain, Portugal, the Balkans - almost everywhere - demons and devils were known in almost every land.

There were almost universal tales of a huge ape-man, seven or eight feet tall, that stands on two legs but runs on four. It dwelt in central Africa and was known as Bigfoot because of its huge footprints - its only known signature and certainly the only proof of its existence.

It was known as the Yeti in far off Asia, the Almas in China and in outlying parts of Russia as Chuchunaa. In the southern Caucases it was known as Dev or as Kaptar. Believed in by many different civilizations of cold northern climes to be a terrible, an abominable beastman of the snows . . .

All these in turn had vaguer counterparts in many lands as it were cloudy mirrors of each others nightmares and dream-terrors that slouched and sloped and loped over the wintry snows of sleepland.

Indeed nightmares seemed to have a

collective invasiveness as though passing from one sleeping soul to another across vast distances. They grinned and grimaced in familiar friendship - shadowy visitants through the dark clouds of the death-horror that has always haunted man as he travels into nightsleep, that brief foreshadowing of the dreaded long sleep.

It seemed to be the rule not the exception that somnambulant beings would flit from dream to dream across the white hills in the common domain of the mind.

Yet there was no zombie, no hint of any creature that even resembled it. There was no body that directly returned from the dead and walked and ate food and drank like living persons but yet remained slow and bloated and foul smelling and dazed like one semi-mordant. No half dead returner, no zombie, in all the literature.

It was a deep mystery. My friend, the antiquarian, had thoroughly checked out the beliefs of the African ex-slaves in the employ of the compounds and no such tradition existed from Africa.

Yet there were rumors of black zombies seen in the far off back hills of New Castile. Why did the myth begin and end here?

Somehow the myth, if that it was, seemed to be connected in popular superstition with physical strength. The black man was strong boned and sculptured by the centuries to withstand a far more severe and savage climate in a land of heat and humidity and rains and ravaging fierce animals and frequent storms and lightning strikes and all the strains put on the human body by the earth's most extreme winds and volcanic explosions.

The Negro had been built up by age-old equatorial forces. How could he be less than a fortress of strength and foresight, destined in all probability to take over from the Indigeno and the white Castile who had been molded by mild and temperate climes?

Here on the Isles of Youth, the occasional storms blew up and blew away but here on the whole was a land of no headaches, no petty illnesses, no dragons, no lions, no elephants - a land on a lower key than Africa.

Yet here, not in Africa, was the zombie - a giant of strength - what was it and why? Yes it was a deep mystery not to be solved from the books of traveler's tales.

Similarly I, Dr. Cohen, although a mere ship's sawbones in my present persona, also prided myself on my knowledge of maxims, folk sayings and popular common sense wisdom yet was at a loss to explain the unique zombie.

It was not in the books of superstitions, yet surely it could not be a true and factual phenomenon and yet and yet what other explanation was there? If it was not a fantasy, it must be a fact. These thoughts more than a little troubled both the sawbones and the antiquarian.

Was magic a reality after all, with its implications of man defying God's chosen destiny?

The royal investigator concentrated his last few days of investigation more for the sake of those judges who would come later, much later, indeed more as a statement justifying his own part than out of any realistic hope of bringing justice to the Admiral.

El Gringo was clearly being found not guilty of any and all atrocities, however well documented.

Yet my friend still the scientific human bloodhound refused to accept magic as an explanation for zombies.

*****

Chapter Thirteen
Why Dogs?

The antiquarian sets out to explain another mystery surrounding the Governor - his strange use of savage dogs.

The basic abiding mystery of El Gringo was why Ferdinand and Isabella's original contract was so strongly, so unbelievably favorable to a foreign adventurer with no money, no experience, no known nobility or family connections - in a word - no hope.

The Admiral's use of dogs was also a great mystery.

The royal investigator, Bobadilla, expounded his thoughts to the hidalgo, Primo.

Forgetting all about El Gringo's malfeasances on the job and assuming that he had been a perfect administrator and that all the allegations against him were a lair of lies, why were the details kept secret in the recent disputes between El Gringo and their most Catholic majesties?

Why were these negotiations settled on such good terms for the Admiral of the Atlantic? Why was there no formal trial, no attorneys for and against, no judge, no tribunal, only a straight whitewash and capitulation by the King and Queen - all powerful in their realm.

Obviously the Viceroy knows too much but what exactly does he know?

What did you think of these ideas Primo? Why use the term Isles of the Sea to describe what is claimed to be a major part of India? India has always been known to be a part of the Continent of Greater Asia.

Kings had always claimed sovereignty over great land masses like India, China, Africa, France, Iberia. Only small princes claimed to own small islands. The Isles of the Blest were a part of the myth of the

Gael, not even the High King of Ireland laid claim to them. Yet Western Isles were now known as a New World. India, of which the Western Isles were supposed to be a part, was an old, old, land. Why call it new?

Of course, the answer might lie in papal law, or as some call it, international law, which demanded that any new sovereignty should be established over new lands - as opposed to those already owned or claimed by Christian monarchs.

This, of course, was in the interests of peace. Under this law, lands belonged to the sovereign, the monarch, who sent out the explorer, not to the discoverer himself or to his chosen, or preferred choice of prince.

Only recently revealed, under great public and church pressure, the original contract between El Gringo before his voyage of discovery and their most Catholic majesties stated clearly that the Admiral, Governor and Viceroy was to be rewarded with 1/10 of all spoils for what he has discovered (past-tense) not for what he might or will or could discover.

This would suggest, as Bobadilla pointed out to the hidalgo Primo, that there had been a previous voyage before the official 1492 navigation.

Some have foolishly interpreted this to mean that El Gringo had been informed in advance by God or the devil - by way of magic divination - of what he would find.

Primo agreed with enthusiasm, "That would explain how El Gringo knew when to expect land. Of course, it was not magic - only factual knowledge of a previous secret voyage - no doubt suppressed and hidden by El Gringo so as to deprive his previous sovereign of the ownership of the isles under papal law.

"Papal law states clearly, as every sailor knows, that all newly discovered lands belong to the explorer's sovereign head of state - not to the discoverer.

"But," Primo continued, "who was the Prince under whom he served in his first voyage and why rob that Prince of a continent whether India or New World?"

Bobadilla replied. "Why? Why not Primo? When you steal, you steal for yourself.

"El Gringo would have had no special contract with his former Prince, giving El Gringo a lion's share of the spoils. His original voyage was no doubt a lucky chance discovery that may or may not have earned a reward of his prince's choice at that prince's discretion. El Gringo was taking no chances and hawked the New World around, disguising his own past and his former name.

"Perhaps he had originally worked for a prince who could not be trusted - a beheader? An infidel? An oath breaker? Perhaps it was all justified? At least their most Catholic majesties were devout."

"Yes, I see it all now," continued Primo, "Who knows? - England, Norway, Holland, Russia, all great sea powers and all non-Catholic. Does it matter? Does it matter, dear heaven? Why, it was a conspiracy to steal two continents. Could anything matter more?

"The two halves of the New World were stolen and given fraudulently to Castile, sad as I am to admit it. As a hidalgo, a loyal subject and gentleman at arms of old Castile, I would have hoped and prayed for better from my beloved sovereigns but no doubt they meant it all for the best - to spread to the New World, the Catholic faith, the only true faith. Yet was that sacred faith to be spread by the greatest fraud and theft of the age?"

Primo became silent and stunned well beyond words as the antiquarian continued our investigative thoughts.

"Now, Primo, we have almost solved the mystery of El Gringo, the Governor, the Admiral, the Viceroy. Indeed, we have totally solved the mystery of El Gringo by basic logic. However, more than logic and common sense is needed. We need proof. This we do not have."

"No, my friend," I interposed, my mind quite at a standstill, my thoughts stultified by the enormity of the mystery and crime concerned, "no, indeed, a man steals a continent twice - once in papal law, from his own true prince and again from the Indigenos who by right of the almighty are the true owners of the new land. And the thief pretends to discover it on his second voyage to the New World so that it will belong to the highest bidder he can find to bribe him. Yes, that makes sense; that is the kind of person he is. It is unbelievable and yet we almost solve the mystery of El Gringo and we have almost proven it all to be true."

But we must also explain the mystery of the dogs, mused my friend. Why El Gringo used Irish wolfhounds, even on his supposed first journey, to drive off the harmless, small Indigenos when Castile swords would have been more in the style of accepted warfare, if indeed force had to be used at all?

Why did El Gringo show such hatred, such fear, such contempt for Indigenos - by all accounts a docile tribe? But if these tactics were necessary, as some argue, how did El Gringo know to bring the dogs with him? Such animals are not the normal tools of war. Why dogs of all creatures? Why not cats or hawks? Dogs always reflect realities in hunting, in fishing or in warfare when under command. Dogs are neat, clean, cheerful and efficient, like their owners, or again like their owners, dogs can be dirty, diseased, undependable rabble, fit only to be put down.

I took up my previous line of thought and continued, "Exactly, there is an old proverb, Know the dog and know the owner. This means his biases, prejudices, hidden agendas and all - for good, or bad. But now we must learn the dog to learn the man - we are almost there. Almost is a terrible, an agonizing thing."

I shook my head in despair, "Almostbutdidn't - the worst dog I ever had. Almost went over a cliff but almost didn't."

*****

Chapter Fourteen

Drums for the Jungle

To solve the final mysteries of El Gringo, the antiquarian gets together a small expedition to probe the unexplored interior jungles of the main island – a place where savage dogs have roamed and where zombies are said to dwell.

Many of the birds of the old world - Europe - are drab in color. Most of the foliage is green - dark or light or greyish - so much so that the Gaelic for green - Glas - is the same word as the Gaelic for grey. Why not - the two merge quite extensively in Europe. So most birds are greyish or greenish or dark brown or black with little dashes here and there of white. Only a few like the robin red-breast, and even he is mostly a drab little fellow, make up a partial exception.

In Europe or Christendom - whatever you wish to call it - it is quite the usual thing to waken up in the morning with a headache, sniffing and coughing with moaning and groaning and stiffness and even pain in the limbs.

This is just everyday life in the old world - drab, achy, stuffy and dull. This is why people long for a new life in a new world. There in the New World, the Isles of Youth or of the Blest - as seen by pre-historic Gaelic sailors - it is unusual to waken up with coughs, catarrh, tensions in neck or back or pains in the back or head.

The air infiltrates and purifies with fresh seaweed, shell-life, clear sea and spring water, woods, bushes, fields and trees, weeds and flowers - the very soil itself - all these fuse into a breathable lung filler that brings health and long life to the New Castilean, the Indigeno and laterly to the African - long life. That is, assuming that no one stabs anyone else to death or hangs anyone else or flogs anyone else to the bone or burns anyone alive in his hammock.

Yes, New Castile is a very healthy place, in and of itself, indeed a paradise of feeling young and blest with calm and peace and healthy living. If only man had gone far away and lived in some other place where he would fit into the landscape more naturally – perhaps the Antarctic - those islands would have been idyllic. But man was here and was to keep on crowding in for many generations to come.

A couple of days after their last meeting, Primo and his minions got together with the royal investigator under the rain-soaked pavilion. Nearby, a rainbow broke out of the sea and then disappeared in the mist and clouds of the archipelago of New Castile. Truly, this was where the rainbow begins. Surely it ends somewhere far away in a calm and balmy valley where old men sing and sip and tip in rocking chairs.

Primo approached the leafy green pavilion where the investigator, Bobadilla, brooded and put together his papers and reread his books and held an open court for anyone or all to come before him. Those who came paid only 1/7 not 1/3 of all their gold and silver, to the Crown and needless to say, they paid cheerfully to the investigator.

"Excellency."

"Yes, my good friend, Primo," the investigator lifted his eyes but they were focused on things, far, far away.

"Thank you, Excellency. I feel the same way - it is a deep sadness that a professional liar and thief and assassin has been set free and is about to return to once again take over these beautiful isles.

"That is why, with your Excellency's permission, I have asked for original witnesses to come forward and speak to you - rather than that I should interview them and then re-explain it to you. I am unable to interpret what I cannot fully understand but your Excellency will be able to understand it all."

"Thank you Primo. Ask them to enter the Court of Investigation."

Primo returned officiously with two Castile gentlemen at arms who saluted the royal investigator respectfully. They were arrayed in full accoutrements of war - from helmet to high-topped boots, from sword to tall, strong axe-head spears.

Following these main witnesses were six friendly Indigenos, small inscrutable dark-eyed and black-haired with bright bronze skins, they carried only the light javelins and daggers of the professional fishermen. Ropes, nets and seaweed got tangled at times and daggers were essential to cut free the men and boys in the light fishing craft of the Indigenos.

Only the Castile officers accepted the royal investigator's invitation to sit at the huge courtroom table; the others choosing to stand and seeming to be more at ease standing behind the ornate high-backed chairs.

"Thank you all for coming here. As you may know I was appointed by Ferdinand and Isabella their most Catholic majesties to be investigator of the Viceroy, Governor and Admiral - the one whom we know as El Gringo. The Admiral - I hardly know, with all due respect, which title to accord to the all powerful tyrant - is on his way back to these - the Isles of New Castile to take over again.

"I will be forced to retire and I fear that slavery and a tax of 1/3, instead of the present 1/7, will be re-imposed. My only hope is to find out something so unconscionable about El Gringo that some powerful interests, other than Ferdinand and Isabella, will come into play against him and then perhaps, just perhaps, someone will be able to stand up against the Governor and replace him with a mere moderate, less greedy, less envious, less demanding ruler.

"Most likely I will not be that ruler. My day is clearly done, but perhaps I can still do some good if I can point my successor in the right direction."

Bobadilla looked at the late-arrived witnesses and with the Castile exception received only polite nods and stunned puzzlement in return. He looked at Primo with the unspoken question, Do they understand?

"Yes, Excellency. They all understand very well - I have explained it to the Indigenos through both interpreters and sign language.

"It is just your Excellency's rapid Castile speech that slightly puzzles them. Taking our time we can make clear every word, if your Excellency wishes."

"Just so," my friend, the antiquarian nodded, but his thoughts were far away where the waves were green sea-weeded hills a hundred feet high, where a boat was a toy slipping and sliding and tossing and tumbling in a great theatre of elemental dramas and plays of gods and kings and mere mortals, a kingdom of armed giants and helpless pawns.

How this turmoil and toil that was suffered by the Castile to get to the New World contrasted with the simple fishing life of the Indigenos. Who was to be envied, even supported, the fisher folk of the New World Isles or the swordswift seasailors from the far off empires of Christendom, with their cross and their crucifixion and their creed of sins forgiven and salvation?

Who was in the right and who was in the wrong? Somehow the answer was not as clear as it once seemed but clear in general was his responsibility to complete his investigation of the great foreigner - the Admiral, Governor and Viceroy. Viceroy - the despotic ruler in place of the despot king - soon El Gringo would be returning to take up his position as an all powerful ruler.

Why? After all his lying and cheating and ripping off the Crown's share, his tortures and enslavements - why, why, why had their most Catholic majesties given this man their total allegiance? Nobility and gentry and peasantry were supposed to give their allegiance to their majesties. Their majesties were not supposed to give their uncritical allegiance to a mere sailor - albeit a master-sailor and explorer.

As these thoughts passed through the mind of my close friend, the antiquarian, unsettling questions jangled back before him to dance and dangle like haunting skeletons of the unanswerable past.

Then he asked the Castile gentlemen-at-arms about the mysterious white men. "I understand you were witness to the capture of Castile sailors by Indigenos. Who were those white men - the Castile - whom El Gringo refused to rescue from the

Indigenos? What was the family home and the name of the captives? Who exactly were they?"

He listened thoughtfully to their responses with a slightly faraway gaze into the future.

"Excellency, the zombies which we saw as soon as we arrived here on our first expedition were white Europeans but they were not captured Castile - they did not even look like Castile - they were not members of our expedition nor were they known to us in any way. That is to say, Senor, these whites were not captured from among our expedition.

"They were already captured when we arrived on our voyage of discovery. They were simply white Europeans, clearly different to us Castile and different also to the Indigenos who had captured them.

"Also, Excellency, they were the living dead, being used by the zombie masters, as beasts of burden, to toil in the fields and hills and jungles and carry home food and water and gold and silver."

The royal investigator considered these statements carefully and silently.

I interjected with amazement, "I am astonished that the whites were not Castile as I have so stupidly assumed. It is truly said, Never take anything for granted."

At last Bobadilla spoke up, "Yes, my friend, I thought that all this was proof of the Governor's callousness but, on the contrary it is proof, far more important, of his duplicity and lies and fraud. He had indeed come here before. This could be important proof against El Gringo. If no other Europeans had come to the New World at that time, those white zombies could only have been El Gringo's previous companions on his first and secret voyage to the New World. Can we find them? Are the white slaves still alive?"

The hidalgo replied, "So far as reports tell - yes they are still being enslaved in the deep jungles to the west on the main Isle of New Castile. Excellency, this is an obscure and remote part of the jungle where very few even of the friendly Indigenos will dare to go"

Primo became a little uneasy and asked the royal investigator.

"Then who will you send?"

"No one – we will all go, Primo – you and I and Dr. Cohen."

"Yes," I agreed. "If you want a thing done do it yourself, if you want it left undone send someone else."

"Indeed Dr. Cohen," pleaded Primo, "Sometimes I fear I am too old for such great treks."

"Never fail to do anything because you are too old, Primo," I remarked philosophically. "Everyone always feels old all the time, for at every moment in life you are the oldest you have ever been and the oldest also that you can have any real hope of being."

"That is true Senor," eventually Primo agreed uneasily. "We never know the moment - especially in a place like this."

Primo at first appeared shocked at my simple common sense but soon recovered, thought for a moment and then continued.

"That is why, dear Doctor, I mention my age because even the young or mid-aged are likely to die in this dangerous, life-threatening El Dorado and I am beginning to run out of middle-age. Where there is gold, there is greed and behind greed there lurks fear and robbery and sword in the back. You are right, Dr. Cohen, age counts for little in such a jungle lair."

"Quite so, Primo." I pointed out. "So, therefore, try to see your age in the light of other people's ages. Consider El Gringo, he is 20 years older than you and see what he can do. Or see your age in the light of your health. A less healthy person, even numerically younger than you is older than you in nearness to death. There is always someone older than you who is unafraid to do what you fear doing. So you might as well do it anyway."

The antiquarian smiled and nodded his thanks to me for my support and then gazed into the far, wet, intense jungles where the white zombies were rumored to walk.

"There, my friend," he said quietly, "is the misty land of the living dead, the steamy lair of the dreaded zombie masters."

"But these Indigenos will lead us. For this I picked them, Excellency." Primo added proudly.

My friend nodded. Then, after some solitary thought while walking alone around the tent and compound, he consulted with his hidalgo as to who would act as adjutant and leader of the Indigenos and Castile.

Together they appointed me as a stalwart ex-military man with good jungle trekking experience. I accepted the honor of accompanying my close friend, the antiquarian.

I, in turn, was instructed to choose and command a good-sized platoon of some 40 well armed fighting men.

The expedition was fitted out with horses, weapons, rations, cooking gear, machetes and ammunition.

The Indigenos also insisted on taking a dozen large wolfhounds, all well muzzled. Four drummers and two fifers were enlisted.

Two interpreters were commissioned for communicating with the Indigeno scouts or any savages whom we might meet.

That night we rested. At the first hint of dawn, the first screech of the early cocks, they set out in good order somewhat to the awe of the more superstitious Castile in and around their camp.

Cheering and waving, they shouted good luck and well wishes to us as their proud comrades stepped out behind the march-beat of the side drummers and fifers who walked behind the royal investigator and me. We, in turn, strode out behind the standard bearer, holding aloft the splendid sign of the Vera Cruz. But soon all this pomp and parade was to change utterly.

*****

Chapter Fifteen
The Dawn That Did Not Come

Deep in the jungles of the zombies the investigator's expedition risks life and limb in the worst form of slavery known to mankind.

Our small troop rode and marched through the grasses and bushes of the low jungle hills where gold and silver were being mined by the Castile with the help of Africans. These laborers were stronger and taller and much better suited than the white Castile to surviving in the hot sunlight of the New World.

However, on this day the sun seemed reluctant to join his friends. Dark clouds streaked with gray and pink replaced the near darkness of the dawn. A brisk, cool wind whistled through the grasslands. Soon the cool wind became cold and a few raindrops fell on the faces of the zombie hunters.

Primo spoke up, "Excellency, there is a jungle murmur that growls messages from one end of the isle to another. It would look bad to turn back. It's obvious that we are intent on a survey or mission of some kind."

"Just so," nodded my friend, pulling over the hood of his cape. "However, the flourish of our departure was not only to encourage our comrades but also to send a false message that we are on a simple, overt, routine mission.

"We will require men of stealth and knowledge and cunning and perseverance rather than fifers and drummers and bannermen. This coming storm is a good opportunity to send back to our headquarters both the horses and the entire band of musicians."

Primo saluted, "Yes, Excellency. I will send them back as soon as the darkness comes."

"Good, perhaps the storm is a blessing in disguise. It may well cover up the sound of our coming to whosoever or whatsoever we come."

The hidalgo nodded, but commented dubiously, "Excellency, can this mean that we are not to take shelter from the storm? Surely . . ?"

"Exactly," I agreed. "Let us all press ahead with our advantage of wind and rain and perhaps, if we are fortunate, soon we will also have thunder and lightning."

"Ah . . Yes . . Of course . . . Let us hope so, your Excellency."

Then I added cheerfully, "Well, let us pray that it will be so, Primo. Prayer is always better than hope. Remember - Better not to begin than to quit without finishing."

"Indeed so, Dr. Cohen."

Our small troop bent their heads into the rising wind, pulling up their hoods and drawing their capes around them like black crows flying into the gray clouds; like deadly druids of doom, approaching a human sacrifice; like monks from dread monasteries setting out to a witch-burning at some desolate windswept crossroads.

To the right and left of our troop, here and there, a few early workers and farmers began their morning tasks gathering or mining but also watching.

"See, Primo," I noted, "we are not alone in our determination to succeed in spite of the storm - Work for the night is coming when man works no more."

"Excellency, I pray, yes I pray that that night does not come upon us unawares." Primo replied with a twisted sideways smile.

Unexpectedly and untypically, the antiquarian suddenly laughed and put his arm briefly across the hidalgo's shoulders, "Wonderful, excellent, you are a true gentleman. You have no need to be a noble. Primo, I am always happy that I chose you as my right hand man, next to my close friend, Dr. Cohen. I could never have made a better choice."

Primo could scarcely conceal his pleasure and gratification but said nothing. What could one say to such praise from one normally so aloof, even cold.

Yet the cold continued to grow all

around us. The wind sharpened and the raindrops splattered more freely. A low, baritone rumble of thunder grumbled innocently in the far isolated distance. Just a polite, genteel, incidental cough, a mere clearing of the giant's throat.

Alas, how treacherous and lying and deceitful can the giant be. Very soon, small colored creatures scurried away to hide and keep quiet lest they attracted the attention of the great monster giant who now roared in the jungles of sea and land.

A sharp lick of the ice giant's tongue spread across the forest hills and slopes on the isle of the cold, cold blast. Rain burrowed into the skin of my little platoon like worms into a cadaver. The gray green giant lit his blinding lamp and it was doused out almost in one second.

Then, angered by the instant obstruction of its light, the monster of the mountain roared his hatred and imminent revenge, trying several times to re-light his lamp with only blinding, sliced-thin blasts of light hitting the fields and hills and gentle slopes like the bright daggers of a revenger stabbing his long-time tormentor to death.

At the same time the tormentor-killer, feeling expiated and satiated in his retribution felt the release of pain but began to realize that even the death of his feared tormentor could not wipe out the tormented one's past. The killer, the ice-giant, broken in spirit that he could do no more to save himself, began to weep bitterly and repentantly.

From the heavens, didn't it rain and rain on the small company and didn't the wind blow from where they were being led, the dark land of the zombie masters.

As Bobadilla, the royal investigator, had foreseen, in part, we arrived in the western jungle of zombie culture without any of the zombie cult denizens being even slightly aware of our presence. For who in their sane senses would dare to travel through such a treacherous and deathly storm?

Indeed, it was true that our little band of zombie hunters were scarcely sane when we arrived in the far hills of the island in the midst of deep undergrowth, looking down on the villages of the zombie masters, as the storm grew weaker.

Peering and peeking through the wet leaves and soggy brushwood of the thick undergrowth we were able to observe some strange but very informative scenes.

Many Indigenos came and went in the villages but some Negroes also lived there. Runaway slaves?

Yet some of both Indigenos and Africans seemed to be slow and cumbrous, even clumsy, in their movements as they went about their heavy handed tasks of lifting, hauling, pulling, carrying - whether water, foods, plants, silver or gold.

Their faces and bodies showed signs of sickness, blotches, bloodstains, whip welts and scars as well as languor and sluggishness.

Their eyes were bleary red and exuding matter. What kind of freedom, what kind of emancipation was this? Was this the stance, the demeanor, the lifestyle of freemen or the blind toil of the living dead?

Yet, other Africans and Indigenos sat around at their leisure and moved about or swung in hammocks without any turmoil or turbulence.

"Just what is going on here?" asked Bobadilla. "I'm afraid I still don't fully understand this enslavement of the zombie. Agreed - the storm is raging on - but it is still daytime - though dark and wet and cold - I thought the zombie was a creature of night? No?"

"No, Excellency. No way. By no means." Primo was worried and serious. "I really did not wish to talk about it too much, Senor, since I still do not fully comprehend it myself. I am not a superstitious person. I go by witness and evidence. Yes, rational proof only is of interest to me, Excellency. So sir that is why I brought along these friendly but also informed Indigenos. Between what they tell us and what we can see for ourselves, we can surely find out the truth of these mysteries. Agreed?"

"Of course, Primo. That is the way to avoid both deliberate lies and superstitions - to put our ideas to the cutting test of observed reality, to slice away all the unwanted growth."

This was an apt metaphor as the

Indigenos hacked their way with machetes, deeper into the remote unfrequented hills of the zombie homelands.

The storm fumed and fretted on with just occasional outbursts of fury but loudly enough to drown out the noise of our platoon's advance. Following in the wake of the scouts and interpreters, the party was led by my friend and I with Primo at our right hand.

As we advanced cautiously, our party continued to catch vague glimpses of distant villages hidden in the wilderness. Suddenly we were signaled to crouch down by the waving hands of the Indigenos. They had come upon a faintly reminiscent scene but much closer at hand than previously.

In a valley below there opened out a misty view of the zombies clearly seen at work. It was a familiar scene. A few Indigeno families sat around warily eating and drinking. Children played regardless. Several men with whips drove both black and bronze slaves about the tasks of gathering food and water and carrying heavy loads. Further off the sound of heavier work, digging and stone breaking could be heard no doubt for silver or gold. The slaves were stiff and slow of movement, their eyes stared and bulged in their sockets and only snarls and groans and moans came from their throats as they were whipped viciously by the deadly eyed Indigeno masters of the enslaved zombies.

It was a scene of simple slavery in what was now becoming a familiar pattern in the steaming jungle except that close up it could be seen that the slaves were more dead than alive.

Their faces were puffed out and covered in sores, their backs were bleeding. It was clear that the slaves, though strong and solid, could scarcely live to a ripe old age, perhaps middle age at most, thus explaining the continual need for more and more slaves and the continual dread of the people for the zombie masters.

Judging by the lack of fear among these villagers, it seemed that they were the families and friends of the zombie masters who, no doubt, sold or bartered their spoils further afield.

Just ahead of our platoon, near the

road, the friendly Indigeno guides had uncovered a shallow grave hidden only by leaves and bracken in which lay the bodies of two Indigenos, apparently dead.

Primo gasped, "So these are zombies. Now that we have seen the zombie at close hand Excellency, it only remains for me to explain to you that, according to my investigations with scouts, our Indigeno friends, speaking to me earlier, the explanation is simple . . ."

"Then my dear Primo, why have you not explained it before? I am quite at a loss . . . I spend much time researching."

"Your esteemed Excellency, I would have explained before but I did not believe it until now. I swear by the Holy Santa Maria."

"Go on."

"Yes, Excellency, it seems incredible, but seeing is believing. A rare and secret fish powder is ground up by the zombie master who leaves it on a plant or path or in a hut, anywhere that the victim will touch. The slightest touch will send the deadly dust into the skin and into the body and blood. The victim enters into a sleep so deep that he is taken for dead. The zombie slave then buried but in a shallow grave covered only with leaves and grasses and tree branches and perhaps some light soil on his body, just like these poor bodies lying here, so that the slave will not suffocate and really die."

Not quite understanding the full impact of all this amazing information, I asked, "Why not, why would the poisoners not want their victims to die, Primo?"

"But Dr. Cohen," Primo gestured to the village in the hollow just below the shallow grave, "your Excellency, can see the answer. It is slavery. They must have their slaves to make wealth and power for them."

"Yes, yes, but why not just enslave them without the zombie dust?" I asked rather naively.

Primo appeared, for the first and last time in his career to doubt the wisdom of his superior.

Bobadilla frowned, "Primo, please continue. . ."

"Yes, Excellency, the victims would resist and fight back - no one wishes to be a slave. They must be zombieized, their minds must become slow with little wit, their bodies must be slowed down, their brains must be damaged by their sleep of two or three or four days. They must be awakened by the slave master who falsely and vilely claims to perform magic from the powers of evil. This power or voodoo, as some call it, is a fraud - shouting and chanting, stamping feet, clapping hands - wakens up the zombie but the slave master does not have real magic. For as your Excellency well knows - there is no such thing as magic?"

Primo's last statement ended on an almost quizzical note.

My friend gazed into the distance and fingered his rosary furiously, then nodded and smiled faintly.

Then he answered thoughtfully, "So zombieism is simply enslavement by means of brain damage. This had been the fate of some of El Gringo's former shipmates, dumbed down by a deadly fish powder to enslave them. These were the white zombies seen being slave-driven by Indigenos when El Gringo returned here on his so-called first voyage. No wonder he took harsh measures . . .

"Of course, Primo, magic is a lie, a cynical attempt to gain power over one's superstitious and foolish neighbors. I am grateful to you for this explanation Primo. You have done a truly great work of investigation and now I understand it all - well almost all - but we greatly progress. What can we do with these poor victims?"

Primo consulted with the Indigenos and the interpreters.

"We can help them out of these shallow graves and take them back to our camp. Their brains will not work well and they will scarcely speak but they can live in peace - perhaps fruit picking or fishing in a slow gentle way - they will be harmless if they are unharmed and unaroused. Only their minds and bodies will be slow because of the long sleep caused by the secret fish dust seeping into their blood."

Primo nodded with self satisfaction.

"Then give the order to carry them back."

"Yes, Senor, and does your Excellency wish to return to our compound. I would agree that we have achieved . . ."

"No, Primo, remember that we came here to rescue white men, not Indigenos, praiseworthy though that may be. Let us press on to seek our friends from Christendom.

"See, the skies are still dark and the storm still whimpers. The winds are still coming towards us disguising our advance. How well we chose only a small party for these narrow ways. Onward my comrades, onward."

*****

Chapter Sixteen

Onward

Now takes place the final last ditch attempt to uncover all the truth about the Governor and Admiral, El Gringo, who went to great lengths to hide his past.

Onward indeed was the cry. As time passed I grew more curious as we paced quietly through the undergrowth, so I asked my friend, "White men to be rescued. I know nothing of this. May I ask who they are?"

"Certainly, Dr. Cohen," he responded. "They are the remnant of El Gringo's secret and unrevealed first voyage. These sailors were captured by Indigenos who enslaved them by means of brain damage.

"If only we can contact them, they alone can tell the story of the Viceroy's first hidden voyage that took place before his well-known so-called voyage of discovery. We need to know the name of the prince they served, for such a prince is the true owner of the New World according to the universal laws of the Pope.

"You know it makes little difference if we find the survivors," my friend murmured quietly to me, "few, if any, will ever believe us or them. It's a case that truth is stranger than fiction."

I nodded tightly in agreement. Just as we stalked stealthily along a narrow ridge and looked down at a wide and gentle slope, we heard the excited shouting of Indigeno voices ahead. It was our platoon scouts. Obviously they had been spotted and sure enough the party caught glimpses of both slow-moving white bodies and fast-moving bronze skins moving through the valley below. Some odd, busy activity was taking place on the part of the half-hidden zombie masters.

A loud barking of wolfhounds suddenly broke out and our huge unmuzzled dogs could be seen bounding towards the zombie-driving Indigenos. These terrified zombie masters dropped small packages on the ground and fled for their lives, hotly pursued by the hounds.

Bobadilla was alarmed and beckoned to an interpreter, "What's going on there? Why have the dogs been unmuzzled and set loose? I gave no such orders."

An interpreter answered, "The scouts have told us that the zombie masters saw us coming and began to scatter the zombie dust all around. The scouts had to set the dogs on them to drive them off and save the party from being burnt by the deadly dust that makes brains die in a slow half-death."

The royal investigator shook his head and I spoke up in near incredulity, "But you and I have long and bitterly blamed El Gringo for using the same tactic. And now we are doing it ourselves by necessity. It is a true saying, There are two sides to every story."

"Perhaps, after all," my friend agreed, "the foreigner had been judged too harshly at least in some ways. El Gringo must have seen the Indigenos use the burning fish powder and later dig up the deep-sleeping victims and capture them as slaves. The problem facing the Admiral was how to scare away the zombie masters before they had a chance to lay one of the most deadly traps known to warfare.

"Perhaps a ship's dog barking had caused consternation to the Indigenos and El Gringo had conceived the idea of bringing huge, savage dogs to the isles on his next voyage - the official one. The dogs were to protect his men and keep the Indigenos and their zombie dust at bay. Their dogs were not there just to terrorize but to drive away a most horrible fate - a living death.

"Truly the great seaman had been dealing with new forces unknown in the history of terror."

"But," I asked my friend anxiously, "my dear friend, what of the safety of the white zombies? Has no one considered them?"

"Your Excellency," Primo answered brightly, "our dogs are bred and trained only to pursue a running quarry. The white slow ones are in no danger."

At this point, the Indigeno scouts rushed back towards the platoon waving their arms wildly and shouting in their native tongue.

Bobadilla asked, "What do these Indigenos mean?"

"Excellency, they are saying no one should proceed because the fleeing zombie drivers have thrown the deadly fish dust on the forest paths to cover their retreat."

"But what of our animals - they are valuable - can they not be saved?" I asked with real concern.

"There is no problem, Dr. Cohen," Primo answered, "the zombie dust does not work on the coarse hair and skin of dogs. Soon they will return safe and looking for praise," turning to my friend, he saluted proudly, "I have investigated it."

The antiquarian nodded briefly in agreement with Primo, "You most certainly have, Primo. So tell me, how can we get in touch with those . . slow white ones?"

"Come, Senor, it will be safe to go just a little ways forward. Follow me. I can see just how close the scouts came to the white ones."

Following in the tracks of the Indigeno scouts, Primo, the veteran explorer of many voyages, led my friend and I to within a few dozen feet of the slow white ones, who walked the forest floor carrying their heavy burdens.

Silent, slavish, bloated, scarred, intense and cumbrous the zombies stared into their eternity.

The antiquarian's voice boomed out into the wet weeping jungle, in a whole-hearted effort to join together the living and the near-dead. The voice carried well in the wet air.

"What flag did you sail under - Catalonia, Russia, Britain, Norway, France? Another? Your ruler should rule these isles. Who are you?"

At times a start, a tick, a flicker of remembrance seem to startle the strained faces of the white ones only to be gone in a split second. On and on they walked into the jungle mists, silently telling a story of fraud and theft and lies and inhumanity with every stride.

The antiquarian shouted after them,

"Who sent you here? Who is your king or queen? Who is your grand duke or earl or prince? Who are you and from what seagoing breed – Viking or Gael?"

"Yes," I joined in, "One, one word only we ask - one word - one name - your king or queen."

Then Primo cried out in agony, "Masters, they cannot answer you. They are the dead of mind - they are zombies."

"Yes," said my friend, "and they are the only real proof of the great foreigner's duplicity. I fear that the zombies will never answer, for the true answers are veiled in the swirling salt-sea mists that close in on these Isles of the Blest, the mists that travel in from the cold northern ocean."

Yet, one last time, the antiquarian raised up his voice to the jungle, "O men of the grave, who are you – Catalan or other Hispanic? British? Russian? French? Dutch? Icelander? Who? One word only." But there was no answer from the grave.

Later, the moon also walked cool and serene; the dogs howled up at her viciously. Deep in the forests the men alive drove their whips upon the groaning and helpless, men half-dead. The zombies trod on and on and on and moaned and toiled under their heavy loads - seeing and hearing little but the sharp shouts of their grim and grinding masters.

And so it is with many and many others for though the great multitudes of mankind do not consider themselves to be slaves yet - neither are they free.

My friend and I began to see only a misty jungle ahead. I put my hand on his shoulder and said quietly.

"My dear friend you alone have solved the mystery of El Gringo – that is more than has ever been achieved by any other traveler or detective."

He nodded and smiled, "As clear as sunbeams, my dear close friend."

*****

Chapter Seventeen

Seahaven Fog – A Peasouper

The antiquarian and Dr. Cohen are back in foggy Seahaven and while they are happy to have solved the mystery of Christopher Columbus there is left on their hands an even more baffling enigma.

The voice of my friend the antiquarian echoed as from a far distance and reverberated in my ear though I could see only swirls of cloud and the foam of high seas or was it all fog?

"My dear friend, this journey of ours has been truly a voyage of discovery in more than one way."

"Absolutely," I replied through the

Seahaven fog that was creeping around his study and bookroom.

The room was empty of my friend and I as we hovered in spirit over the study of his seaside abode.

Had this adventure been a case of true time travel or was it interdimensional crossover?

Perhaps we had suddenly snapped into a place of vision in a deep sleep, a strange landscape free of time or place?

Or perhaps we had been somehow reunited for a short spell into the personas of our former selves in a previous incarnation?

After we had found ourselves seated once again in our favorite chairs, we talked about the experience we had just been through and came to different tentative conclusions.

I told my friend the antiquarian that I believed it may well have been time travel. He smiled and nodded thoughtfully as he thought hard about the event for some time. Then he finally told me that he was pretty sure that it had been just a telepathic tandem dream.

After some 40 years of close professional and indeed our uniquely creative partnership he believed that we really were on the same wavelength.

I was flattered but puzzled by the possibility that it could have been a transdimensional crossover. As for time travel, we had not disturbed the historic pattern, nor interfered with history in any way.

My querulous thoughts were that our sea voyage may have been based on many authentic accounts, either by fellow mariners of the great discoverer, or based on the behavior of real persons. Or was it possibly based on the spiritual logic of the historically proven real-life actions of those who acted over again, the events of times past?

Perhaps the study in Seahaven, is a place of crossover between worlds. There are places of crossover where one can step from dimension to dimension. Had we found a field-stile leading to the past?

I pointed out to my close friend that we could indeed have just been dreaming. But how could we both have been doing real things and have shared our complimentary actions so closely?

Was it a case of old men's dreams coming true or was it a case of a joint telepathic vision based both on my friends investigative instincts and on his deep study of the real voyage of Christopher Columbus?

Perhaps this may be an example of an abstract, spiritual situation of great import where the elements of the universe have seemed to lean down upon us and to briefly move us into a different dimension in order to improve our understanding and our enlightenment of our own and other worlds. Was this all a warning that we should not credit man's puny, erroneous and revisionary view of history? In this case, history could be seen as mere fictional, self-serving propaganda – strictly to be avoided in the interests of truth.

Yet, in the entire Adventure of the White Zombies, as I had thought of entitling it, the name of Christopher Columbus was never used throughout the entire voyage. This springs to my mind something I once read about an infinite number of parallel universes where intensive thought, study or prayer can briefly transpose one to a close resemblance of our present world reality at the exact moment of identical development in the parallel planet's history.

Certainly, in the first place, my friend the antiquarian had been concentrating his powerful mind on the study of the mystery of Christopher Columbus and his thoughts could well have been intense enough to project us into such a shadowy alternate existence.

Perhaps most strange was the fact that we both remembered all the details of the adventure, as clear as daylight – not as from a misty dream. Indeed, when we woke up in our separate chairs in the study, back in Seahaven, we bore no trace or memento of our visit to the isles, the ship or seas of New Castile.

Neither clothes nor suntan nor weapons nor artifacts survived. Our usual English had been the language of the entire adventure.

At this point my friend remarked, "You realize, my dear Cohen, that many of the events on our voyage actually happened under a royal investigator named Francisco de Bobadilla?"

Then I, Dr. Solomon Cohen, shook my head in wonder and remarked to my old friend.

"And this is entirely based on the truth that you have so meticulously researched."

After further discussing all these enigmas I was dumbfounded and put my head in my hands.

"How could it all have happened?" I asked, still in some shock.

Stretched out in his armchair, my friend smiled slightly, "Yes, it's a mystery. It seems that we have solved the mystery of Christopher Columbus but now we are faced with another mystery about which we will never discover the solution, my dear Cohen."

"Well," I replied, calmly, "As the Irish say – Never is a long day and I have a shivery suspicion that one day, beyond these passing days, one day further along we will know more about it. Already we understand where, what and who and when.   Further along perhaps we will understand the how and the why."

He nodded, "Well said, my dear Cohen, but that must be at the time when all of life's mysteries will be solved. I'm not sure whether I would want to see such a day."

As we relaxed in our armchairs, I seemed to see battle armor, the palm trees, colored birds and jungle greenery – wraithlike images of swarthy suffering faces – indigenous sailors and Spanish adventurers in treasure islands of long-ago and faraway or perhaps nearer than we think?

In the Seahaven fog?

--The End—

Did the Antiquarian and his friend solve the mystery – What do you think?

www.ingramcontent.com/pod-product-compliance
Lightning Source LLC
Chambersburg PA
CBHW071715140626
46557CB00011B/267